It Wasn't Me

CREINA MANSFIELD

THE O'BRIEN PRESS
DUBLIN

First published 2001 by The O'Brien Press Ltd,
20 Victoria Road, Dublin 6, Ireland.
Tel: +353 1 4923333; Fax: +353 1 4922777
E-mail: books@obrien.ie
Website: www.obrien.ie

ISBN: 0-86278-696-7

1 2 3 4 5 6 7 8 9 10
01 02 03 04 05 06 07

The O'Brien Press receives assistance from

the arts
council
an chomhairle
ealaíon
50+

Editing, typesetting, layout, design: The O'Brien Press Ltd.
Cover illustration: Royston Knipe
Colour separations: C&A Print Services Ltd.
Printing: Guernsey Press Ltd.

CONTENTS

To Alex, with love

1

It Was Worth a Try

'Do I have to go to school tomorrow? Can't I have a day off to settle in here?'

No answer from the kitchen, although Jack thought he heard his mum snorting at the suggestion. She was still unpacking, and Jack heard the clinks as she unwrapped pieces of china and placed them on the kitchen dresser.

He tried again. 'It's a big thing – moving from the country to the city. I need to adjust.' Then he had one of his brainwaves. 'If I had a day off school, I could sort out my room.'

'Oh, yes, that's what you'd do, is it?' He'd finally got his mum's attention. She stood in the kitchen doorway with her familiar half-smile on her face. 'So you wouldn't spend yet another day in front of that thing?'

'That thing' was the PlayStation he'd been playing all day Sunday. He was up to level 5 on the latest Formula One.

Jack bent down to rub his dog behind the ears. 'Jasper, if Tiger Woods had my mum, she'd have told him to stop wasting his time on the golf course!'

Jasper was resting companionably on Jack's left foot. His brown eyes gazed sympathetically back at Jack.

Jack tried again. 'This is teaching me how to drive. You'll thank me when I'm seventeen and don't need any lessons.' Jack would be seventeen in six years' time – six years with Jack, Mum and Dad, Jasper and the cat Basil, now settled, or at least living, in Dublin. Six years, thought Jack: a life sentence. To Jack, moving to Dublin was like being sent to prison – with no parole.

'Seventeen?' His mum raised her eyebrows. 'You think I'm going to let you drive when you're seventeen? One maniac in the family is quite enough for me, thank you!'

'Get a load of this, Mum!' Jack took the controls of his virtual Formula One racing car. He sped away, accelerating sharply. Soon he was driving at over 180 miles an hour as he swung expertly round the racetrack bends. The whine of the engine increased as he saw his main rival, Michael Schumacher, ahead of him.

Boldly, Jack increased his speed even more. He drew level with Schumacher, and leaned forward in perfect concentration as he revved the engine and overtook him.

Jack jumped up, punching the air above him, and sent Jasper diving behind the sofa. 'Yes! Record time! I'm completely unbeatable!'

Jasper crept out from under the sofa, and Jack grabbed

his head in an arm-lock and grinned at him. Jasper circled Jack in celebration. Just for a moment Jack forgot about Dublin, the pokey new house, the walls closing in, the strange smells and noises and, worst of all, the new school looming up like a brick wall in front of one of his speeding racing cars.

Mum was used to Jack's brainwaves, or 'diversion tactics' as she called them. She just didn't fall for it this time. 'Well, you're still going to school tomorrow,' she said, returning to her work in the kitchen. Calling out from there, she added, 'I know it's a new school and you're a bit scared. But we've talked about this, Jack. You'll soon get used to it. You'll see. Anyhow, it's a very good school.'

Quietly, so Mum wouldn't hear, Jack told Jasper, 'It's a dump …'

Jack's head felt heavy, his tongue dried out and he had that creeping feeling up his back he kept getting lately. He made a fist with his hand and knocked the PlayStation controls to the floor. Why did they have to move, anyway?

Jack knew the answer. His dad had to change jobs. And Jack had heard the 'moving lecture' often enough: 'Sure, it was all a bit difficult – moving house, changing schools. But it would be worth it in the end – more money, a better future for them all.' Jack's brain told him it made a kind of sense.

But that didn't stop the anger – or that creeping feeling. *They* didn't have to face a new dump of a school with no friends. It was all right for *them*.

Jasper tilted his head and gazed sympathetically at Jack.

'Come on. I'd better go and pack my bag. I'll only get the lecture again,' complained Jack. He moved slowly, limping slightly, thirty kilos of golden retriever having numbed his foot.

2

When 2 and 2
Should Equal 5

Jack was thinking of his friends as he neared the school gates. There was Michael O'Farrell, fanatical about computers and ready any day now to hack into the files at the Pentagon, or so he said. The Kirby twins, who didn't have a good word to say about each other – not until someone else had a go at one of them, and then each would fight to the death for the other. Paul McBride, who could tell you who played for Manchester United any time in the past thirty years but who bunked off all games classes because he hated exercise …

His friends – odd, yes, but *his friends*, and he no longer had any of them around. Hundreds of miles away, they were going through the familiar gates of St Michael's, whereas he was here at Penrock College, heading under the impressive wrought-iron arch with its Latin motto. What did it mean, anyway, Jack wondered.

'Welcome, Suckers!' he guessed, knowing how much Mum and Dad were paying to send him to the school. Something about the place impressed them to the point of madness. They were always telling him who'd been to the school years before. Politicians, pop stars – a load of people they actually *disliked*, in fact. But now he was meant to think it was some sort of privilege to be following in what Mum called 'the hallowed footsteps of the Great and the Good'.

'Hallowed' must be different from 'hallo' because no one had spoken to him yet. Jack stood alone in the playground, leaning against the wall like he didn't care.

So far all he knew for certain were the names of the other boys in his class, though the way they answered their teacher gave some clues to personality. There were a few who looked stupefied when their names were called. Perhaps they were surprised to find themselves there at all. Teacher: 'Brian Mallet?' Again, 'Brian Mallet?' Boy with blank look on his face: 'Er, yes … I mean, yes, sir.'

Then there was Ronan Hart, who shouted, 'YES, SIR!' so loudly when his name was called that the teacher would say caustically, 'Thank you, Ronan!' This couldn't subdue Ronan for long, Jack noticed. Ronan was the sort of boy for whom a sharp pencil was an offensive weapon. There wasn't much Ronan – or 'Ronny' to his friends (grand total: two) – felt he shouldn't comment on. He had leadership qualities, which meant if you didn't do exactly what he said, you found yourself upside down in a dustbin with his henchmen ramming you up and down to take a few inches off your height. Few in the class escaped his attention, and Jack was determined to keep a low profile. 'Concentrate on your studies,' had been Mum's advice. If only life was that simple …

Trouble had started during maths class. Mr Abbott, the teacher, had told them all to work out factors. Jack had done factors at his old school, and he even knew a few short cuts. After explaining factors, Mr Abbott gave the class ten questions to work out. Ronan objected, 'You mean *now*, sir?'

'Of course, Ronan,' Mr Abbott replied briskly, well used to Ronan's time-wasting techniques.

As they started to work he paced about the classroom, leaning over to look at their calculations. They worked well for him, but they were relaxed. Mr Abbott had taught them geography as well as maths since they'd first started in the school in September. His loud voice and manner were familiar to them, so even when he found Ronan gazing out of the window with a blank sheet of paper in front of him and shouted, they weren't worried.

Going close up to Ronan's left ear, Mr Abbott began in a stage whisper, 'It must be very annoying when you're just sitting relaxing and people come and BUILD A SCHOOL ROUND YOU!' He barked the last five words into Ronan's ear so loudly that Ronan complained, 'Ouch! That hurt.' But he picked up his pencil and started scribbling.

Having jumped when Mr Abbott shouted, Jack quickened his pace. He didn't want to be the last to finish. He worked frantically, finishing the ten sums before some of the class had reached question 3.

Mr Abbott was pacing up and down the aisles. He stopped next to Jack and picked up his maths book. 'Well!' His finger traced down the line of sums. 'This is, as the poet said, "sweaty haste".' Some chortles at the word 'sweaty' but most of the class waited to see what impression the new boy was going to make on Mr Abbott. 'Every calculation complete,' said the teacher with approval.

'Bet he's got 'em all wrong,' snorted Ronan.

'Let's see how many Jack's got right, shall we?' said Mr Abbott, keeping Jack's book open in his hand. One by one he gave out the answers to the sums. There were yells of 'Yes!' when someone got one right. Mr Abbott checked Jack's answers, saying, 'Correct!' each time.

Ten times he said, 'Correct,' and each time Jack heard a groan from Ronan. Jack's palms were getting sweaty and the creeping feeling was starting up his back. He began to hope for a wrong answer.

'Excellent!' boomed Mr Abbott, throwing the book down triumphantly. 'How did you do them so quickly?'

'Well,' Jack began. He didn't like the looks he was getting from Ronan and his pals, but on the other hand he didn't fancy Mr Abbott bellowing in his ear either, so he continued, 'A number is a factor of a larger number if it's a factor of the sum of the digits.'

'And have you done highest common factors as well?'

'Yes, sir.'

'So if I asked you what the HCF of 12 and 21 is, you'd say?'

'Three, sir.'

'Well done!'

There were sarcastic 'oohs' and 'ahs' from Ronan and friends, who were staring at him with threatening grins.

'What's so great?' asked Ronan. 'He learnt it before. He's from the country. They haven't got anything better to do there.'

'So the only hope for you, Ronan, is to put you on a desert island and leave you there!' snapped Mr Abbott.

Ronan scowled and he continued to scowl as Mr Abbott went on and on about intelligence, concentration and application. No one was actually listening, certainly not Jack. All he heard was a price being put on his head; all he could feel were hundreds of spiders racing up and down his back; all he saw was the inside of a dustbin getting closer and closer ….

Finally Mr Abbott finished. 'The application of knowledge, lads! That's what I call intelligence!'

Ronan waited until the teacher had returned to his desk and was out of earshot before he added, 'That's what I call being a smartarse!'

Jack was meant to hear and he did. I wish I'd shut up, he thought to himself. Why couldn't I just have made 2 plus 2 equal 5?

3

Cornered

The second week of school began, and, reluctantly, Jack returned. He had kept quiet after the maths class disaster. Every day he had run home after school hoping it looked as if he had somewhere to go, someone to see.

Most of the class seemed OK, in fact, but Ronan had made it clear that the first person to be friendly to the newcomer would become closely acquainted with the inside of a dustbin. Jack stood alone at breaktimes and had not yet found his way to the canteen at lunchtime. As every day passed, the speed at which he headed through the streets that led to and from school increased.

'For heaven's sake, slow down!' Mum warned. 'They're real cars out there, you know. You'll be *in* heaven at this rate!'

And when he got home there were the PlayStation, television, Jasper and Basil for company. There were no open spaces, as there had been in what Jack still thought of as *home*. When he'd looked out of his bedroom window there, he had seen open fields. Now he stared out on other terraced houses.

Jasper was also having trouble adjusting. He missed the big garden and the long walks along country lanes. He was busy establishing new comfort zones and his favourite was the bottom bunk bed in Jack's room.

The bunk beds had been one of the new bits of furniture needed because of the move. Instead of four large bedrooms they now had two, plus a tiny boxroom. Mum hadn't been keen on buying the bunks, but Jack had got his way on that one. They didn't really need bunk beds but Jack liked the idea of having another bed in the room, in case someone needed it as well as Jasper. Now and then Jack played a game where he imagined he had a brother lying in the bottom bunk and he acted out their nighttime conversations in his head. He liked lying close to the ceiling – it was the safest place he'd found in Dublin so far. Nights were spent listening to Jasper's heavy snoring below.

Basil, who was slowly adjusting to the transformation in his territory, chose a spot by the side of Jack's desk for his Significant Space. With Jasper for company, Jack returned to the world of blowing up scientists with remote mines, carrying a RCP90, or, as James Bond, saving the free world. It was that or telly.

'You're becoming addicted,' declared Dad as Jack sat in front of the television on Sunday afternoon. 'Ever since we moved here, you've done nothing but stare at that thing.'

Dad lit a cigarette. 'What you need is some fresh air.' He inhaled deeply and blew the smoky air out of his mouth.

Jack coughed elaborately. 'Going out, then, Dad?' he asked.

His father stared at him for a moment. 'No, son, *we're* going out,' he corrected, sounding very determined. A fine spray of ash fluttered from the cigarette in his hand as he grabbed his jacket.

'Come on,' he ordered, then called out to his wife, 'Marie, we're going out for a while! We're going to suss out the area.' He slapped Jack on the back; he was being exaggeratedly, alarmingly cheerful. 'OK? We're going to case the joint. That's what you youngsters say, isn't it?'

'If you also happen to be a criminal.'

'Come on,' urged Dad. 'Best foot forward!'

'You mean we're going to *walk*?' asked Jack, genuinely shocked at the idea.

The ceiling shook as Jasper, hearing the word, bounded off the bunk and headed down the stairs. He was to be disappointed. Dad drove everywhere. Outside of the house, to see him walking was to witness a mini-miracle. He loved his metallic green Golf and seemed more at ease behind its steering-wheel than anywhere else. He was a strong man and stockily built, with short legs, probably because he didn't need them. Witness evolution at work.

Dad shook his head, ignoring Jasper's forlorn expression. 'No, of course not! We'll take the car. Then we'll have it if we need it,' he added, giving his usual excuse.

The beloved green Golf was parked outside number 27 Avondale Road. Jack and his parents had moved into number 13, but ever since Dad had returned from work on Friday evening to find a white van parked outside his house, his car had been down the road. Dad tutted as he made the marathon journey from number 13 to 27. 'All these cars even on a Sunday!' he complained. 'Who do they all belong to?'

'The people inside the houses?' suggested Jack.

'Well, it wasn't like this in the country,' said Dad, throwing his fag end into the gutter before unlocking his car.

As they drove away, Jack wondered what Dad meant by this. Everyone he could think of in the country had a car. They had to, if they ever wanted to go anywhere. There was no public transport, no DART. Jack knew this stood for 'Dublin Area Rapid Transport'. Did they have a similar system in Frankfurt? he wondered. If so, they'd better not call it the 'Frankfurt Area Rapid Transport' …

Suddenly Dad was shouting, 'Come on, missus, don't take all day!' He was yelling at the driver of the oncoming car who'd quailed at the sight of the Golf bearing down on her at speed in a narrow city street. She'd stopped ahead of them, unsure whether both cars could pass. This exasperated Dad. He hadn't been able to touch his toes for years, but as a car driver he had the flexibility of a Chinese acrobat. As the woman driver dithered, Dad drove forward, one hand lightly on the wheel, swung to the left of her car, missing side mirrors by a centimetre, then shot away in top gear.

This was all too familiar to Jack to merit comment. Dad had driven like this all Jack's life. Mum had told him the story of when he was born. There'd been some sort of emergency, so she'd been rushed to hospital in an ambulance, with the siren going.

'But when your Dad collected us a week later, he drove faster than the ambulance had!' she had told Jack.

Now they drove round their new neighbourhood, pointing out to each other the shops that stayed open late and the likely dog-walking areas. 'Trouble is, these roads all look the same,' complained Dad.

'Not if you're walking,' countered Jack. He was already growing familiar with the intricate network of alleyways that ran behind the houses and also linked Avondale Road to Patrick Road, and Beaumont Road to both.

'There's a park through those gates,' said Dad, pointing. 'You'll be able to take Jasper in there.'

Jack did all the dog-walking.

'Do your friends use that park?' asked Dad as they sped on.

'What friends?' asked Jack, but Dad was too busy overtaking on the inside through a bus-lane to hear.

As they turned towards Avondale Road again, Dad pulled up suddenly. 'Hop out and get me some cigarettes,' he said. There was a shop on the corner cleverly called 'The Korner Shoppe'.

'It's against the law,' Jack reminded him. 'You go.' He liked to have the car to himself. He could work the pedals – more preparation for the day he was allowed to drive.

'There's nowhere to park,' complained Dad.

Jack hadn't realised, of course, that the law said children must not buy cigarettes *unless there was nowhere for their dads to park*.

'Here's a fiver. Can you find your way home?' Dad asked, barely letting Jack get out before he drove away.

Reluctantly Jack entered the shop, trying to decide how to attempt the illegal purchase. In the country he'd bought cigarettes for Dad lots of times. The first time he had turned up at the shop asking for cigarettes for his dad, he had been only ten, but Mrs Sullivan hadn't minded. She had known Jack all his life and approved of sons running little errands like this. It might be different here.

He approached the counter. The assistant was a young, bored-looking guy. So far so good!

Jack was about to ask for 'Twenty Rothman's please,' when he heard a voice behind him. 'A factor is the sum of the larger number if the digits in the factor are.' It was Ronan with his gang, Brian 'No Brains' Mallet and Colm 'Cock' Roche, as Jack had christened them. They were like dogs tagging along beside their master – 'No Brains' the big bloodhound and Colm a squirmy whippet. They sniggered at Ronan's imitation of Jack's maths.

Jack didn't know what to say. He turned back to the assistant, who was staring at him, which was the closest he was prepared to come to asking a customer what they wanted to buy.

I'm surrounded by nice guys, thought Jack. Now what?

He hesitated. Buying cigarettes in front of Ronan might not be smart. Ronan might:

A inform their class teacher, or

B want the cigarettes and take them.

A would make Jack's life at school even more difficult and **B** meant Dad would be down five pounds and twenty cigarettes. Quickly Jack stuffed the five-pound note into the front pocket of his Levi's and, without acknowledging Ronan's presence at all, left the shop.

He started running as soon as he got outside, and was soon at the end of the road. He turned left, heading for the alley that linked Beaumont Road and Avondale Road.

But Ronan and his pals knew the area too. They knew a short cut and were waiting for him! They circled.

Jack thought of dustbins, and gulped! His back was crawling. He looked at the unpleasant trio and asked, 'What's your problem?' He was tempted to add, 'Apart from chronic acne and low IQ,' but he hoped to avoid violence if he could.

Ronan managed, 'You're the one with the problem, maths boy!'

Jack stopped himself from reacting to the reference to the maths class. How he wished it hadn't happened, not with him there in the middle of it. That was the trouble with life. When you wanted a friend, you were on your own, but when Home Alone was an attractive option, you got surrounded by morons. He wished he wasn't in the street, having to defend himself against this lot.

Then it occurred to him. He wasn't there – not Jack, perpetrator of the unforgivable crime of knowing some maths. He was someone else, tougher, smarter. As coolly as he could he asked, 'Do I know you?'

Ronan's lips curled. 'No, Jack, you've never laid eyes on us before,' he said sarcastically. 'What are you on about?'

'Jack?' Jack repeated, wondering if some sort of foreign accent would help. Could he pretend to be someone from France, or Somalia, or St Louis, USA, who just happened to look remarkably like this Jack? Michael O'Farrell had gone on about Doppelgängers. Everyone had one, apparently – someone so similar that no one could tell them apart. Michael had met his getting off the bus to Tralee. They were like identical twins, he had said.

'Yer in our class,' prompted Ronan's sidekick, Colm 'Cock' Roche, almost helpfully. Ronan scowled; this wasn't meant to be a conversation. He was ready for action.

Jack made a move towards Avondale Road, but all three blocked his way.

'Oh, I see!' Jack tried to look as if the very simple, quite amusing really, explanation of what was happening had just occurred to him. 'You're getting me mixed up with my brother!'

'Brother!' repeated Ronan, backing away a little.

'Yes,' Jack faced them as he moved slowly backwards towards Avondale Road.

'You've got a brother that's as ugly as you are?' asked Colm.

'Of course!' Jack decided to ignore the 'ugly' jibe. 'We're identical twins!'

He had the satisfaction of seeing gawps of surprise on their faces before he turned and ran. If he'd waited around any longer, they might have decided that it didn't matter which twin they roughed up.

Jack only stopped when he'd reached 13 Avondale Road and was safely indoors. Jasper greeted him by jumping up and licking his face.

'Get my cigarettes?' asked Dad.

'Didn't sell them,' said Jack, reaching for the five-pound note and handing it back.

'It was a tobacconist's!' objected Dad, bright as a button when it came to nicotine supply. Really, what did Dad want? His only son had escaped from the streets without having his face rearranged, and all Dad cared about was his own nicotine craving!

'Not your brand, and … they wouldn't sell them to me. Underage, you see,' explained Jack, ruffling Jasper's coat to distract from the weak story.

Fortunately Dad bought it. 'Too many damn regulations, if you ask me,' he moaned. 'I thought this was a free country. Why don't they do something about all this street crime we keep seeing on the telly?'

'Seeing on the telly!' Jack repeated as he and Jasper headed for his room. 'Take my word for it, Jasper. It's a lot nearer than that!'

4

Jack's Brother

'Can't I stay off school tomorrow?' asked Jack. 'I'm feeling a little queasy.' Grandma had got plenty of sympathy when she'd felt a little queasy at his cousin's wedding. Nobody'd expected Grandma to go deal with a bunch of morons!

'You ate two plates of roast beef, a whole apple crumble and you've had two Mars bars, I'd be surprised if you didn't feel queasy!' was all Mum said. When he was younger, she'd panicked whenever he seemed ill. She used to fuss around him all the time until one day Jack exploded. Since then she'd backed off a lot. Nowadays, it was Jack who sometimes wished he had more of her attention, though he'd never tell her. He knew it sounded soft but just sometimes he'd have liked someone special to talk to – not just a friend.

Since the move his mum seemed really preoccupied with the house. Even now she was busy complaining. The dust from all the cleaning had irritated her eyes and she was wandering about without her contact lenses, screwing up her eyes like Oddjob in *Goldfinger*.

'Little queasy' wasn't going to do it, Jack realised, reflecting on the injustice of life. Jasper had, in fact, eaten the second Mars bar (sucked, with the wrapper still on). Getting off school was going to mean *starving* himself. His mother would only have herself to blame if he became seriously ill, he decided, grabbing a third Mars bar.

So he was going to have to face his tormentors. Still, if not Monday, then it would happen Tuesday. They'd still remember. Unless … unless he could contract some illness that would keep him off for weeks.

A strategy was required if he was to get out of school. He needed an illness, preferably highly contagious and requiring a special diet of four meals a day plus as much chocolate as he could eat. There must be something that you caught in the country and it developed when you got to a city.

He could use a red marker pen and cover himself in blotches. It was an old trick but it just might work. He might need to work on a puking strategy as well. Wasn't newspaper in your shoes meant to make you sick, or should he try a finger down his throat? A bit drastic, thought Jack. Maybe he could go out and find some sick. There seemed to be plenty of it on the city streets.

Jack nearly did feel sick by this stage. He was grossing himself out. Still, he had to try something. Here goes, he thought, and he started to prepare the ground.

He went into the kitchen where Mum was finishing the

washing up. 'Mum, I'm really itchy,' Jack complained, scratching his arm.

'Fleas!' shouted Mum. 'Quick, grab Jasper while I get the powder!'

'But it might not be fleas,' objected Jack as Mum frantically shook powder over a reluctant Jasper.

'Now catch Basil,' said Mum, ignoring him.

'It doesn't feel like fleas, more like chickenpox,' said Jack.

'You've had that as a baby and you can't have it twice,' Mum told him. 'Unlike fleas,' she added as Basil wove casually past her on his way to his food bowl. 'Quick, grab him!' she yelled.

Jack did so, and Basil's claws were immediately out.

Mum shook the powder vigorously over the cat as he climbed over Jack's shoulders onto his back, every step marked by claw-marks in his skin.

'Good, that's done!' said Mum as Basil leapt from Jack's back, and Jasper watched them sorrowfully from his basket.

So much suffering and nothing had been achieved, Jack thought as Jasper continued to stare accusingly at him. All the diseases in this world and he'd chosen the one he'd had as a baby and you couldn't get twice!

That was that. He would have to go to school and face Ronan's questions about his identical twin brother. How did he manage to dig himself such a big hole? And wasn't it a sign of madness, thinking you were two people, like Dr Jekyll and Mr Hyde?

But *he* didn't think he was two people! He wasn't the mad one: it was these psychopaths he had to deal with – idiots who bore a grudge because you knew how to do maths. If he started to get his schoolwork all wrong, then Mum and Dad would start complaining about the money they were wasting on his education. If it were up to him, the money would be spent bribing the authorities to allow him not to go to school.

Face facts, Jack told himself:

1 You have to go to school.

2 There are at least three psychopaths there who hate your guts.

3 You have already told them you have an identical twin brother.

Fact four is – and this is crucial – *you have no twin brother*! What were you thinking of? Jack asked himself. Those three might not be the brightest creatures on two legs. Actually, he knew brighter creatures on four legs, he reminded himself, giving Jasper a pat, but even morons like Ronan and his gang were not going to forget what he had said entirely. They would want to know his brother's name, where he went to school ...

There was no other choice. He simply had to have a twin brother and that was that.

Fortunately, the Kirby twins at St Michael's were identical so he had something to work on. At first, no one in the class had been able to tell them apart. Then they had noticed that one twin had a mole on his left cheek and the other hadn't. Also, as they'd got to know them better, it was obvious that one was more daring than the other.

OK, the braver *his* brother was, the better! He needed not just a brother; he needed a psychopathic brother!

'So, shall I have the mole?' Jack asked Jasper. 'Mum and Dad don't notice much of what I do, but even they would notice that.' So my brother will have to have the mole, Jack decided.

It sent a shiver through him, putting those words together. *My brother*. 'I went fishing at the weekend with my brother.' Or, 'My brother and I went to the football on Saturday.' Even 'The brother and I argued about what to watch on telly' had a warm, comforting meaning to it. It was a bit scary how right that felt. Weird, thought Jack. Maybe when you really start imagining you are two people it sends you crazy!

He forced himself to concentrate. If I had a brother, I'd want him called Jasper, thought Jack. So, *Jasper* it was. 'Do you want a mole?' he asked the golden retriever. Jasper seemed to interpret this as an offer of a second helping of flea powder and backed away.

Jack grabbed a brown felt-tip from his schoolbag and ran to the bathroom to try it. He'd better make sure he always got the mole in the same place. Looking in the mirror, he marked a point on his left cheek directly under the side of his eye and in from the lobe of his ear. He considered the effect critically. Hmm, it was OK. But it was fairly obviously made with a felt-tip and when he tried to remove it, he had to scrub so hard that his skin was red. He might need to remove the mole in a split second, to transform himself. He'd seen a film once where hard lads who'd been in detention centres gave themselves little tattoos under the eye. Jasper would have a mole like a borstal mark.

He took down his mother's make-up bag and found the sticky pencil she used to make her eyebrows look darker. He drew on the mole in the same spot. Excellent! He stood back and surveyed the results with satisfaction. Hello, Jasper, spitting image of Jack, but formidable, ready for the mean streets around Avondale Road.

'Jack?' Dad was watching him from the doorway.

'I was feeling a little queasy,' said Jack, 'and I was looking for something for a little queasiness ...' Jack trailed off, wondering just how long his dad had been there.

'Well, you won't find it in there!' said Dad, staring oddly at the make-up bag and the eyebrow pencil. Then he asked, 'Found any friends to play football with yet?'

'Not yet, Dad.'

'Might be a good idea,' muttered his dad.

5

Threats

'Right, to work!' said Mr Abbott briskly on Monday morning. It was geography. Jack had been forced to take a front desk and he felt Ronan and his pals staring at the back of his neck. Now he really did have that creeping feeling up his back.

He was beginning to have serious doubts about this twin thing. I've got no choice, he told himself, trying to listen to Mr Abbott go on about projects at the same time as anticipating Ronan's next move. By now, Jack was wishing like mad that Jasper really would appear.

'... begin preparing a project,' the teacher was saying. 'Yes, there is a prize.' He anticipated the first question. 'Projects mean prizes! What do projects mean, Brian?' Mr Abbott asked.

'Projects mean prizes, sir!' shouted 'No Brains' Mallet, grinning and flashing the gap from his missing front tooth.

That creeping, crawling feeling was running up and down Jack's back like mad.

'And this project is to be on the environment.' Mr Abbott charged to the board and wrote the word in letters six inches high. 'Notice it's got an "n" in the middle of it. I don't want any work on the enviro-ment.'

A stream of questions followed.

'Can we work on card?'

'Yes.'

'Can I do hedgehogs?'

'Yes.'

'Can we work in pairs?'

'Yes, but no more.'

'Can we use scrapbooks?'

'Any form of presentation, including dance and mime, is acceptable.'

A tall boy had started pirouetting around the room.

'However, by the end of this lesson I want to hear from each of you what you are going to investigate and how. Thank you, Andrew!'

The boy stopped pirouetting and grinned widely.

Jack noted that the class, including Ronan, clapped rather than jeered. *He* wouldn't have risked doing *that*. Andrew must be popular, or a good fighter – possibly both.

'Can we do drawings?'

'Of course! Any *sensible* questions?'

'Can we work together?'

'I've already answered that. Listen, then I won't have to

repeat myself. Right, off you go.'

Jack risked looking round to count the class. There was an uneven number, so if everyone chose to work in pairs, he'd be the odd one out. If they weren't talking to him, they could hardly work with him.

The boys ambled about the classroom, taking the opportunity to waste some time whilst 'thinking' about what to do for their projects. To Jack, there was an obvious subject. It had occurred to him as soon as someone mentioned hedgehogs. Jack had pictured a hedgehog on the city streets, desperately trying to manoeuvre amongst the traffic. It wouldn't last five minutes!

'Saw you yesterday.' Ronan had sidled up. He looked no friendlier than the day before.

'Where?' asked Jack, stalling.

'You know where!'

Colm 'Cock' Roche had wheedled up to join Ronan. 'Yeah, you know where!' he echoed, stretching his scrawny neck out to the side like a demented bird.

'So which is the organ grinder and who's his monkey?' asked Jack.

'Listen!' hissed Ronan. 'Cock' Roche stood in front of Jack to block Mr Abbott's view.

'You can't run away all the time! We know where you live!' He kicked Jack's bag across the room towards 'No Brains', who kicked it further away.

'I take it that this is a discussion about the environmental project?' asked Mr Abbott.

'It's not safe around here, sir!' said Ronan, still looking at Jack.

'What was that?' asked Mr Abbott.

'Yes, sir!' said Ronan and Colm in unison.

'So what have you chosen to do?'

'Haven't decided yet, still thinking, sir.'

'Oh, Ronan, if I believed you were *thinking*, I'd be a happy man,' said Mr Abbott as he guided Ronan and Colm back to their places. Then he returned to Jack's side. 'And have you decided yet, Jack?'

'Yes, sir.'

'What have you chosen?'

'Cars, sir.'

'Excellent!' Mr Abbott's powerful voice quietened the room. The class listened as he went on. 'Cars have an enormous impact on the environment. I mean, look at this!' He'd gone over to the wall where there was a black and white photograph of the school. 'When was this taken, anyone any idea?'

'About 1940?' suggested someone.

'Not a bad guess. 1933, actually. And you notice?'

'No cars, sir,' came a chorus of voices.

'Exactly! This place has been transformed by the motor car. *We* might be transformed by the motor car!' He stopped and smiled. 'But I'll let you reach your own conclusions. I don't wish to sound anti-car. I am the proud possessor of one myself.' He pointed at a brand-new BMW in the car park.

'Are you interested in cars?' he asked. He was speaking directly to Jack.

Ronan was mouthing 'smartarse' at him.

I seem destined to impress this teacher, thought Jack. He'll be telling them all I'm a genius in a minute and I'll end up losing some teeth.

Then a thought struck him. He smiled as he said, 'Me and my brother are, yes, sir.'

'You have a brother? Which class is he in?' asked the teacher.

'He's not in this school, sir.'

'Is he younger than you?'

'We're twins,' explained Jack, suddenly wondering why he had started this and feeling he was falling into a great black hole. 'We're identical twins,' he added, making sure he didn't look at Ronan, Colm or 'No Brains'. Telling the teacher upped the stakes. It gave his story more credibility, but it also meant it was more difficult to retract.

'Interesting! We usually keep twins together,' said Mr Abbott.

'Mum and Dad thought it was time we spent some time on our own,' explained Jack, 'on account of us being so much alike.'

'Ah, I see,' said the teacher, giving Jack a curious, or was it a questioning, look. 'Easier for us anyway. Identical twins can be ...' The bell rang. 'Final project choices by next lesson, please!' said Mr Abbott as they left the classroom.

As Jack followed the rest of the class to the next lesson,

someone grabbed his neck from behind. 'So what's wrong with this twin brother of yours, then? Wouldn't they let him into our school?'

'Give it a rest, Ronny! You know they'll have anyone here.' It was Andrew, the boy who'd pirouetted in class. 'After all, they haven't thrown you out *yet*.'

He karate-chopped Ronan's hand off Jack's neck.

'I'm just being nice to the new boy,' objected Ronan, shaking his hand to cool the stinging.

Andrew faced him, still smiling. If it comes to a fight, thought Jack, I'll have to wade in. He came to my aid. But Ronan hesitated for a moment, then swung away.

Jack slid off down the other end of the corridor. He couldn't risk hanging about to thank Andrew. He needed to get away to do some thinking. Now he had told Mr Abbott and the whole class about his identical twin brother, he would have to be ready with some answers when the questions started.

6

Collision

When school ended, Jack had to go to the school office to buy a school tie. The headmaster came out of his office just as he was rolling the tie up and stuffing it in his pocket.

'Ah, the new boy!' said the headmaster breezily. 'Settling in nicely?'

A few answers came to mind. What is your definition of 'nice'? Is 'settling in' a reference to the fact that I may soon be getting to know a dustbin really well?

However, the headmaster didn't wait for an answer, so Jack's sickly smile was all that was required. The headmaster sailed on down the corridor, happy to have done his duty. Jack shook his head, wondering at the gullibility of headmasters.

He checked his watch: 3.50pm. Ronan and his pals could all be waiting in ambush by now, Jack realised. He slipped out of the school gates and started to run home. He had worked out a reason why he and Jasper were not at the same school, but he would delay answering any more questions for as long as he could. At this game, he was still at level 1.

He sped home. He was beginning to know the small alleyways that threaded through the rows of terraced houses. It made his journey quicker to take these, and, he hoped, safer.

He reached the last alley leading onto Avondale Road and was looking forward to the safety of home. Just as his thoughts turned to what was for tea, he collided with a shape so solid that he bounced backwards and fell, landing on his side and scuffing his arm. He looked up, scowling, expecting to see Ronan smirking at him. When a hand reached forward, Jack automatically shielded his face with his arm.

'Hey! Take it easy!' It was Andrew, the pirouetting Andrew.

One single, unrepeatable word had been uttered by Andrew as Jack hit him, but he was smiling now, grinning in fact, as he surveyed the results of the collision. Although he had stayed on his feet (good balance, thought Jack), the bag of tomatoes he had been carrying lay scattered and squashed on the gravel path. Only one was intact.

'Look at that!' said Andrew admiringly, picking it up and brushing the gravel off on his sleeve. Then he asked, 'What are you doing – training for the next Olympics?'

'Sorry, sorry about the tomatoes.'

'At least these are OK,' said Andrew, holding up a

carton of cigarettes. 'Granny can have the tomato and these for tea!'

'They're for your gran?'

'Yeah, she lives over there,' explained Andrew, pointing to Avondale Road. 'I do her shopping. Live round here?'

'Yes.' Jack pointed to the other side of the road. 'Number 13.'

'This is my gran's house – number 62,' said Andrew. It had dull, peeling brown paintwork and lace curtains heavy with dust. The small front garden had tall grass behind an overgrown hedge. 'Do you want to come in?'

Jack nodded and followed Andrew up the path. There was a saucer of milk by the front door. Andrew took a key out of his pocket and unlocked the front door. As he did so, he began yelling, 'IT'S ME!'

She must be deaf, thought Jack, as he followed Andrew in. The air was suffocatingly stale and Jack tried not to inhale. He recognised a particular smell. Ah, yes: the pleasant odour of used cat litter.

An old lady entered the room. 'Hello, luvvie. School all right today?' She had two cats weaving between her frail legs as she shuffled in.

'FINE, THANKS, GRAN,' shouted Andrew, smiling and nodding at the same time.

Jack bent down to one of the cats. It arched its back slightly and pranced slowly past him. All it took was a gentle 'hello' from Jack and the cat turned to be petted.

'Samson's taken to you,' said the old lady approvingly.

She chuckled, 'He doesn't like many people.'

Jack, still kneeling, looked up at the old woman. He did not have to look far; she was incredibly short. Jack stood up. As he thought, he towered over her. Her back was so curved that her neck and head seemed to sprout from half-way down her body, giving her the look of a bird of prey. Grannysaurus, a rare beast, thought Jack, laughing to himself.

'THE TOMATOES GOT BROKEN,' shouted Andrew.

'Who? Whose toe's got broken?' asked his grandmother, looking worried.

'NOT TOES, TO-MA-TOES,' yelled Andrew. He picked up the one remaining tomato and started to mime. First, Charlie Chaplin walking along, looking about him, carrying the tomato. Then, along comes Jack, running like the wind. Suddenly, crash! Andrew slapped his hands together to convey the collision, and the old woman understood. Jack laughed at the performance.

'Oh, he broke my tomatoes!' she said. 'And now you've broken that one, Andy.' In slapping his hands together, Andrew had smashed the final tomato. The two cats were already sniffing inquisitively at the juice running between his fingers.

'Whoops,' said Andrew. 'I'll get a cloth,' and he went out into the kitchen.

Jack waited, smiling at the old lady and watching the cats. He could not think of anything to say that would not sound absurd at the volume he would have to use for her to hear it.

Andrew came back and began to clear up the tomato juice on the floor. As he did so, yelling began on the other side of the wall.

'What's that?' asked Jack.

'That's Cuthbert, the man at number 60,' Andrew explained. 'He's always yelling. Lucky Gran's deaf, so it doesn't disturb her. BUT YOU DON'T LIKE HIM CUTTING YOUR ROSES, DO YOU, GRAN?'

'Who's got a neurosis?' asked Gran.

'I SAID THAT CUTHBERT CUT YOUR ROSES,' Andrew tried again. Then to Jack he explained, 'He'll pick a fight with anyone. He's drunk most of the time. Some days he just stands at the door and shouts at anyone who's passing. The milkman won't deliver milk there.'

'Don't suppose he drinks much milk, though,' said Jack, thinking it would be more of a punishment to this unpleasant-sounding character if he was *made* to drink milk.

That reminded him. 'Does your gran want some tomatoes? My mum'll have some.'

'Great! My mum'll kick up a fuss if she thinks I haven't got Gran her tea.'

Andrew shouted, 'JACK'S MUM WILL BRING YOU SOME TOMATOES, GRAN.'

'What?'

He repeated what he had said and added, 'YOU CAN OPEN THE DOOR TO HER, GRAN. IT'S OK.'

'Oh, I'm not nervous,' said the old lady unconvincingly. The yelling went on in the next house, and Jack wondered if, despite her deafness, she somehow sensed the unpleasantness on the other side of the wall. Then she said, 'Samson scratches him next door, ever since he threw water over him,' and Jack thought, she can tell what's going on.

After Andrew had cleared up, the two boys left his gran smoking a cigarette.

'She's leaving all her money to her cats, Samson and Rosalind,' Andrew told Jack as they walked towards number 13.

'No way! Really?' Jack shook his head in disbelief: Grannysaurus, direct descendant of Completely Battyrex. 'How much?'

'No idea. She thinks it will make them safe. She can't bear anyone hurting animals. I had to stop her watching *Pet Rescue*. She was always crying.'

'Cats don't like water,' added Jack, imagining how Basil would take it if water were thrown over him.

They had reached number 13. 'Hey, I've suddenly thought ... if you hadn't been wearing school uniform, I wouldn't have known if it was you or your twin.'

'Em, no.'

'Are you, like, completely identical?'

'People say we are,' said Jack reluctantly. 'They're always muddling us up.'

'So looking at him is like looking in the mirror?'

'Sort of.'

'So … if you saw a photo of one of you, would you know if it was you or him?'

Jack hesitated. He'd sound loony if he said he couldn't recognise himself in a photo, surely. Reluctantly, he explained, 'Well, my twin's got a mole just here.' He indicated his cheek. 'So fortunately people who know about it can tell us apart.' He was desperate to change the subject. He was just about ready to tell Ronan a barefaced lie, but not Andrew who was being so friendly.

'So he's got a mole there and you haven't? What's his name, by the way?'

'Jasper.'

'Jasper,' Andrew repeated. 'OK, Jack, see you tomorrow!'

'Yeah!'

'Oh,' said Andrew, turning back, 'do you want to do that project together?'

'Sure!' Jack was pleased, but he would have been delighted if he had not lied. It seemed a mean thing to do to the first friendly person he had met. He went to his house, wondering how to get out of the mess he'd got into …

7

Cousin Frank

'Have you been fighting?' Mum asked as soon as she saw Jack. 'Your jumper's all mucky.'

'No, I just had a collision.'

'What! You *have* been fighting!'

'No, I mean I ran into someone – a boy in my class. By accident. His gran lives on the other side of the road. Mum, her tea got spoilt. Can you take her over some tomatoes?'

'I'm not sure I've got any.'

'Something, 'cos she's really old and *frail* ...'

'What number does she live at?'

'Sixty-two. I don't know her name,' said Jack, anticipating the next question. 'She's Andrew's gran and she's going to leave all her money to cats.'

'She's lucky to have any to leave!' laughed Mum. 'Anyway, guess who's coming round here?'

'The President? The Pope? Frankie?'

'Yes, he phoned earlier. I knew he would,' said Mum

fondly, as if making a phone call was as self-sacrificing as donating a kidney to a stranger. She always spoke like this about her sister's son. She had her sister Pat's belief that Frankie could do no wrong. Now he was training to be a lawyer, and the family were already storing up legal cases for him. Had he been a High Court judge, the twenty-one-year-old would not have had the power or wisdom that his family believed he had already.

'Great! Frankie's coming round!' Jack liked his cousin Frank; it just was not for the reasons Mum and Aunt Pat thought. *They* saw Frank as the 'Great Guiding Example'.

'Work at your studies like Cousin Frankie,' Jack had been told since he started school. Frank had attended the school Jack had just left, so, with a ten-year gap between, he had been following the same path. Some error had occurred that had led to someone other than Frank being chosen as head boy but, nevertheless, he had got into UCD to study law, and Jack had been left in no doubt that he should follow. A further mistake had occurred when Frank failed to get a brilliant degree, but he passed and the whole family had attended the degree ceremony. Mum was dressed like a wedding guest, dabbing her eyes with her hankie every now and then, Dad was red-faced and beaming with pride, but all Jack could think about was his cousin's legendary school career.

There had been the bookmaking racket. Frank took bets on everything from who would win the Murphy Memorial Trophy (given for outstanding public-spiritedness) to the length of the bishop's speech on Prize-Giving Day. He calculated the odds in maths class and paid out on a Saturday evening. Aunt Pat said all the visitors just went to show how popular her Frankie was – another reason he should have been head boy. Then there'd been the slightly more questionable sale and purchase of essays … Jack smiled to himself. Sometimes parents can be incredibly stupid – even more stupid than normal.

'Jack, Jack, did you hear me?' Mum interrupted his memories. 'I said I'm going out to buy some things for the meal and I'll drop in on the old lady. I want to feed Frankie up. Your Aunt Pat thinks he's working too hard and neglecting himself.'

Jack managed a sympathetic 'Oh.' He immediately wondered what scam was taking up Frank's time now.

However, Jack never uttered a word of what he knew to Mum or anyone else. In the Mafia, they call it *omertà*, the vow of silence, even under pain of death. It existed for Jack and Frank. If Andrew became a real friend, it would exist for them too.

Jack sighed. How could you pledge *omertà* to someone who lied to your face? He should have trusted Andrew. He was digging his way into a bigger and bigger lie, and for what benefit? What good was brother Jasper going to be?

The doorbell rang and Jack raced to answer it. His cousin was there, grinning down at him. Frank had straight dark hair that flopped over one eye. He was handsome, though he had a crooked nose that had been broken when he was playing rugby for the school.

'Welcome to Dublin!' he said cheerfully to Jack.

As soon as he was through the front door, Jasper was jumping up and licking him while Basil wove through his legs. Mum, when she returned from shopping and visiting number 62, was scrutinising him for signs of malnutrition, and Dad was waving a six-pack of his favourite lager under his nose. Jack would have to wait for his share of his cousin's attention.

While he waited, and they ate the meal Mum had lovingly prepared, Jack tried to work out just why he did like Frank, despite knowing that 'Frankie the Great Example' did not exist. To start with, there was no malice in Frank. He would not turn on you just because you knew more about factors than he did. With the ten-year age gap, Frank had had plenty of opportunities to torment his little cousin, but he had never taken them. He had never twisted Jack's arm up his back, stolen his sweets or used his advanced skills of mother-manipulation to get the better of Jack. He'd always taken it for granted Jack was an OK guy and on his side and he just trusted him.

That was it, Jack decided. Frank had a sort of optimism, a generosity of spirit. Perhaps he was a Good Example after all …

'Borrow it whenever you like,' Dad was telling Frank. 'I know you'll treat it OK.'

Mum nodded in agreement. 'We know you're a responsible driver.'

'Thanks, you're really great!' said Frank, and he sounded like he meant it.

'But be careful with the parking,' Dad warned. 'It's a nightmare around here!'

'Yes,' Mum agreed. 'You have to manoeuvre into little spaces.'

'I think I'll manage,' said Frank modestly.

I bet, thought Jack as he remembered the time Frank reversed the drama teacher's car through the double doors of the school hall. It had been found parked neatly next to the grand piano.

Frank turned to Jack. 'Any new games on the Play-Station?'

'Lots. Grand Prix Racing's pretty good.'

'Give you a game!'

While Mum and Dad cleared up, the cousins played Grand Prix. Then, when they were alone, Frank asked, 'How's the new school?'

'It's a dump!'

Frank raised his eyebrows. 'Why?'

So Jack told him about Ronny and his gang. 'I've two serious problems: One: how to avoid the interior of a dust-bin, or worse, and two: everyone is too scared to talk to me, except one big guy, Andrew.' Jack did not mention his invented twin brother Jasper.

Frank looked at his cousin carefully. 'Listen, I had a similar situation when I went up to secondary school. I did not grow much until I was fifteen, so most of the boys were bigger than me. Some of them tried to bully me.'

'What did you do?'

'What you have to do is … get them before they get you. It's the classic brains-versus-brawn scenario. Pick the opportunity, don't talk to them, just march up and beat the cr… Crikey! Is that the time?'

Mum and Dad had walked in from the kitchen.

Frank looked at his watch. 'I have to go. I've got an early lecture in the morning.'

'Now, don't work too hard!' Mum cautioned him.

'After that meal, I'm ready for anything. Auntie, you are an even better cook than Mum! And thanks for the offer of the car, Uncle Phil.'

'Let me drive you back now,' offered Dad.

'It's too much hassle,' objected Frank.

'No, it isn't! Let us do it. I'll come too,' said Jack. He needed more time with his cousin even if Dad would be listening.

So, when they were in the car, careering through the Dublin streets, Jack asked, 'What you were telling me earlier – Frankie, what do you do if, you know, there's just you?'

'Be observant … that's the secret of good driving, isn't it, Uncle Phil?'

'Sure is,' said Dad, speeding along in the bus lane.

'And pick your time and place.'

'OK.'

'Look for the weak link. This car is only as strong as its weakest component.'

'The nut behind the wheel!' said Dad, thinking he was joking.

'Find the weak link and snap it.' Finally, as he got out of the car, Frank turned to Jack, ruffled his hair and said, 'Remember, planning! Prepare your move and execute it.'

'Yes, thanks.'

'A great lad,' said Dad, admiringly, as they lurched away. 'I hope you're going to take the advice he was giving you about your work. Did you listen?'

'Yes, Dad.'

'Frankie's got a real future ahead of him. I can see him, in a few years, in the Central Criminal Court, can't you, Jack?'

'Yes, Dad.'

Jack could picture it too. He just was not sure whether Frankie was sitting on the bench in wig and robes, or in the dock, in handcuffs …

8

The Weak Link

Jack swung the hurley stick above his head, holding it firmly with both hands. Twice it whizzed round, and then he jabbed it forward. It caught the edge of a swimming trophy on the shelf and swept it off. The trophy flew through the air, smashing against the bedroom door, leaving a gash in the paintwork.

'What *are* you doing up there?' shouted Dad from downstairs.

'Nothing. Just practising!' Jack picked up the swimming trophy (a life-saving award) and replaced it on the shelf.

'Yes, but practising what? Demolition?' Dad's voice was coming closer. He had reached the landing. Jack could hear him muttering something about 'breaking the house down'. Harassed-parent alert!

Quickly, Jack jumped up and hung a pair of jeans on the hook on the door, to cover the mark that the trophy had made, and slid the hurley stick under the bed.

Dad entered the bedroom. 'When you've got your own house, I'll come round and kick your furniture!'

'You'll be very welcome.'

'Don't be smart!'

'I thought I was meant to try to be smart!'

Dad looked at him carefully. 'What are you doing up here? Jasper and Basil came haring down the stairs when there was that crash.'

Jack shrugged. 'Just thinking.'

'That's the noisiest thinking I've ever heard,' complained Dad. 'Why don't you take Frank's advice? What was it?'

'Plan. Prepare your move. Execute it.'

'Great advice!' said Dad. 'Come on down and watch some telly with me. Come on,' he urged, 'or Mum'll watch *Coronation Street*.'

'OK,' Jack said, willingly.

Jack had spent the weekend thinking about Ronan's gang in an attempt to identify the 'weak link'.

Colm, Ronan's echo, wore glasses. One well-aimed blow with a hurley stick, and Colm would be having them surgically removed from his nostrils. Was that the sort of thing Frank meant? Maybe a little lacking in subtlety.

Ronan, Jack had noticed, took a different route after school, unless he had some serious intimidation planned, for which of course he needed company. He was on his own all the way home. Some of the route was through similar alleyways to the ones around Avondale Road. That made him vulnerable.

And then there was Brian 'No Brains' Mallet, the third member of Ronan's gang, and a hot contender for the Stuupidest Person in the World Contest. Unfortunately 'No Brains' was a muscle man. He was easily the tallest boy in the class. He had long, hanging arms and a head that jutted forward. He looked more like the Missing Link – half-man, half-monkey – than the weak link ...

Downstairs Mum was sitting watching the adverts.

'What's on?' asked Dad, as if he didn't know.

But Mum wasn't fooled. 'Watch whatever the two of you want, so long as it isn't guys doing guy things,' she said resignedly. By this she meant sport. 'With other blokes commentating on them in stupid voices,' she added bitterly. This was a familiar complaint of Mum's, who claimed to be outnumbered four to one, because even the pets of the household were male.

They could agree on watching *Inspector Morse*. The programme was about a detective who seemed to think that he knew everything, and nobody else knew anything, just because he had a degree from Oxford. In this episode a grisly murder had taken place and Morse was called in to do his stuff. The victim had been beaten to death by a blunt instrument. A hurley stick, perhaps?

Jack decided it might be a good idea to leave the hurley stick under the bed.

As usual, Mum and Jack tried to solve the murder. Mum picked out the character with the meanest expression but Jack was fairly sure it was not that simple.

'I like *Colombo* better,' interrupted Dad. 'You can work out who did it.'

'They *show* you who did it,' Jack pointed out.

'I like his style,' insisted Dad, who was losing the plot of *Inspector Morse*.

'You've got his dress sense,' teased Mum.

It turned out that the murderer was the secretary. She wore a wig when she drove to do the murder so that any witnesses would give a misleading description.

Good move, thought Jack.

Jasper was lying on Jack's foot, watching TV with him as he often did. He looked up as Jack patted his head. Could Jack turn Jasper into a ferocious animal, who'd look like he'd tear you limb from limb? No chance, thought Jack. Anyone who knew anything about dogs could tell that Jasper was of the non-biting variety. Shame about that, thought Jack. I've got more chance of persuading them my twin's violent!

Jasper, of course! Not four-legged Jasper, but identical twin brother Jasper. He could do the serious damage. That was better than a wig – it was a full-person disguise! But he had to work out who was the weakest link.

Jack patted Jasper. 'You are the weakest link!' he said, imitating Anne Robinson's voice.

'That's an unfair game!' complained Mum.

'Yes,' Dad agreed. 'They often pick the strongest link.'

'What?' asked Jack.

'The others don't choose the person who isn't doing

well. They choose the one who is,' Mum explained.

'Makes sense, of course,' said Dad. 'Go for the threat.'

Of course – Ronan was the weakest link *because* he was the leader! It was Ronan Jack had to go for, then the rest of the opposition would crumble. Jack smiled to himself. Now he had worked that out, what to do to Ronan was the simple bit.

The next day, he began preparations. He joined the drama club.

9

The Plan

'So what's this idea you've got?' asked Andrew.

'Idea? Me? I haven't got any ideas,' said Jack.

'Well, one of us better think of something or we'll fail!'

'Oh, the geography project! Sorry!' said Jack, wondering what Andrew's reaction would be if he added, 'I've been busy planning how to ambush one of our classmates.'

Sympathetic, possibly.

'I think we should find out how often people use their cars and for what sort of journeys,' suggested Andrew. 'See do they really need them or is it just laziness.'

'A survey? Good idea. How do we do that?'

'Don't know. Bunny'll tell us.'

'Who?'

'Bunny – Mr Abbott. His name's Ray Abbott. R. Abbott, Rabbot – rabbit – so we call him "Bunny".'

Jack could see Brian Mallet watching him and making throat-slitting gestures as Andrew talked. 'We'd better ask

Bunny how we plan a survey, then,' he said. He was actually starting to wish he could think more about schoolwork!

At the beginning of the geography lesson Bunny had an announcement to make. 'This is a reminder from Mr Daley. All of you involved in the forthcoming musical, please remember there is a meeting after school tomorrow – in the sports hall.'

'A musical!' shouted Ronan. 'What – like *The Sound of Music*?'

'This year Mr Daley has chosen *Annie Get Your Gun*,' said Bunny with a smile. 'How many of you are involved?'

Not a single hand went up.

'Anyone interested?' Bunny asked. 'I understand there are still parts to be had.'

Jack was thinking. The last thing he needed was to volunteer for some play with a girl's name in the title, but what he did need was a good alibi. He needed everyone to know where he was, or to think they knew where he was, when he carried out his plan. Bunny asking publicly like this was an opportunity he wouldn't get twice. Slowly he raised his hand.

'Thank you. There'll be none of that,' said Bunny briskly as the hoots of derision from Ronan's gang began. 'Jack, you're interested?'

'Will the rehearsals be after school, sir?' asked Jack, hoping the teacher would remember his question later.

'Yes, Tuesdays and Fridays, so I understand.'

'Then I'll go along,' said Jack.

Ronan and his pals stared in disbelief. They were already giving the new guy a hard time and he delivers ammunition to them as a gift.

'He'll probably get the part of Annie,' yelled Ronan, to laughter from his cronies. 'I mean he's good enough to get the lead,' he explained unconvincingly to Bunny, who gave him a stern look.

'Well done, Jack. Getting involved in after-school activities is always worthwhile,' said the teacher, approvingly.

It had better be, thought Jack, bearing the stares of the whole class, including Andrew.

10

Preparations

Jack made sure he left school as soon as the bell rang. The last thing he needed was to be set on by Ronan and Co. before he was ready. Mr Abbott knew he was going to the auditions for *Annie Get Your Gun* the next day, so that decided when he had to act.

When he got home, Mum was in a good mood. 'I went back to see the old lady at number 62,' she told him. 'It felt funny, not knowing anyone in the street. Now I'm starting to get to know people.'

'Mum, you haven't thrown out my old school blazer, have you?' asked Jack. His plan depended on his St Michael's blazer.

'It's hanging in your wardrobe,' Mum answered absent-mindedly. Fortunately she was intent on telling him what had happened when she had met Andrew's gran. Jack had realised, too late, that inquiring about his school blazer could be evidence against him.

'So, you met Andrew's gran?'

'A remarkable woman!' Mum shuddered. 'Her house is a bit … you know … but those cats are wonderful! Rosalind is just like one of the first cats I ever had. And what about your day?'

'All right. I'm going to audition for a musical tomorrow.'

'You're going to do *what*?'

'Audition for a musical.'

'I didn't know you enjoyed singing.'

'I don't.' Another wrong move. What was he doing auditioning for a musical if he didn't want to sing? 'I mean, I don't *yet*, but I think I might.'

'Well done! Always good to try something new,' said Mum cheerfully.

I'm going to do that all right, thought Jack.

'What do you want for your tea? Poached eggs?'

'NO!' He needed those eggs. He couldn't risk his mum running out.

Jack spent the evening going over his plan and checking everything was ready. Getting through the next day at school was going to be difficult.

When he got to school, he found Andrew was still the only person in his class to talk to him, unless you could count 'No Brains' Mallet running round him with his arms outstretched singing 'The Hills are Alive to the Sound of Music'.

'So you want to be in *Annie Get Your Gun*?' asked Andrew, sounding interested. 'Do you like singing?'

'Sure!'

'Perhaps I should come along ...'

'NO!' Jack didn't need company at the auditions, though he realised, as he said no, that Andrew was probably saying he'd come along to be supportive. He was certainly popular in the class and Jack could do with some of that popularity rubbing off on him. 'I mean, thanks, but you visit your gran after school, don't you?'

'Sometimes.'

'I'll let you know if it's any good, OK?'

'Sure,' said Andrew.

As the final bell rang, the would-be actors started making their way to the hall. Jack followed them, his schoolbag slung over his shoulder. It contained his St Michael's school blazer and six eggs.

It took some time for Mr Daley, the drama teacher, to achieve some sort of order, as the younger boys slid on the polished parquet flooring and shouted at each other. It was a chaotic scene that suited Jack well. Perfect! he thought. And when the drama teacher explained how he was organising the auditions, that fell nicely into place too. He was going to start with the major roles and then deal with the minor ones. Sixth-year boys were auditioning for the star roles, so they were up first.

'It could be an hour or so before I get to the rest of you, so if that causes problems for anyone, let me know. Now, I want you all to sign up for a role in the chorus,' said Mr Daley. They had to sign their names on the lists, choosing between 'Chorus of Indians', 'Chorus of Society Ladies and Men-About-Town', or 'Chorus of Bystanders, Cowboys, Wrestlers, Tumblers, Clowns, Roustabouts and Layabouts'.

Jack signed his name for the last of these.

'And you boys, don't go too far away! I don't want to have to send out search parties for you when you're required. But KEEP THE NOISE DOWN! Get on with your homework, or do something constructive, if you can manage that!'

I hope so, thought Jack, as he quietly slipped out of one of the side doors.

He ran out of the school gates. Jack had calculated that Ronan and the gang would stay together for twenty minutes or so, idly chatting and looking for victims. Now, if he ran like the wind, he would catch Ronan up in the alleyways.

Jack ran through the streets, his heart thumping. When he reached the first alleyway, he stopped and took out the mauve St Michael's blazer. He ripped off his tie and jumper and put on the blazer. Then he took out the eyebrow pencil and drew the mole on his cheek.

He ran on. Yes! There ahead of him was Ronan – alone, sloping along, deep in unpleasant thought.

Jack drew back, then turned and ran along the alley parallel to it so he could get ahead of Ronan at the other end. He felt determined but also a little nervous. The most difficult thing was to pause before entering the alley and stand there waiting. He pulled the carton of eggs out of his bag, took a deep breath, turned and walked purposefully into the alleyway.

Ronan still had his head down, so the first two eggs hit him before he had even seen his attacker. Jack was pleased with the accuracy of his aim. The third was even better, hitting Ronan right on the nose. Egg yolk and slime slid down his face.

'What the …?'

Jack never stopped walking. His pace never varied. Smack – there went the fourth egg. As he drew nearer, it got easier to hit his target. And his target did nothing to defend himself. He stood there, stunned, his mouth gaping. That was a mistake, as it gave Jack the chance to ram the fifth egg into his gob. It didn't break, so Ronan looked like the rear end of a chicken.

'Now listen,' said Jack, 'you give my brother any more grief – you can work out who is my brother, can't you, you cretin? – give Jack any more trouble and next time it won't be eggs that'll hit you!'

Jack took the final egg and put it inside Ronan's shirt.

'Remember, we shoot vermin in the country!' As he said 'shoot', he smashed his hand against the final egg.

Ronan stared at him. The egg fell from his mouth and his lip quivered. Jack felt a glimmer of sympathy, but held his gaze and moved forward.

Now it was Ronan's turn to run, and he did not stop until he was out of sight. Jack stood in the alley, listening to the departing footsteps, the empty egg carton in his hand.

11

Jack the Roustabout

Jack slipped back into the sports hall, out of breath. He was just in time to hear Mr Daley read out a list of people in the chorus as roustabouts. His name was there. Jack had no idea what a roustabout was, but he didn't care. It didn't sound like a girl's part and he had his alibi. Mission accomplished!

'Did you get a part in the play?' asked Mum, as soon as he walked in.

Gee, I wish she wouldn't jump on me like that. Jack was all nerves these days. 'Yes!' he said, and all the satisfaction he felt at Ronan's running away came out in his answer.

'Well done!' said Mum, clearly delighted. She called through to the sitting room, 'Jack's in the school play!'

'We should get net curtains,' came the curious reply. Jack and Mum looked at each other in confusion. Jack made a face, indicating that his father had finally lost it completely.

Mum giggled. 'He's obsessing again,' she told Jack, raising her eyebrows.

'Whatever for, dear?' she asked, humouring Dad.

'Then we could look out without anyone seeing us.'

'You are not still watching that car, are you?' asked Mum in exasperation.

'It shouldn't be parked outside our house! I've had to park right up the road!' complained Dad. 'I'm going to talk to Frank if this goes on – see what the law can do.'

'You haven't got a legal right to the space outside your house. Even I know that,' said Mum.

'Yes, but morally, ethically …'

'It's a parking space, dear. They're not mentioned in the Ten Commandments!'

Jack grinned. Adults lived lives of such simplicity and innocence! Fancy Dad worrying about a parking space!

'Anyway, Jack has some good news. Tell him, Jack.'

'I've got a part in the school play.'

'In the school play? Excellent! What part?'

A tricky question. Jack shrugged. 'Dunno. A rouster-something …'

He should have found out what a rouster-something was. Now he'd be interrogated.

'What do you mean you don't know? How can you play the part *with conviction* …' Mum was going all Meryl Streep on him, 'if you don't know who you're playing?'

Dad tried to be helpful. 'Say again what it is.'

'A rouster, something like that …'

'A rooster! You're playing a chicken!' said Mum, astonished.

Now they were driving him mad again. 'It's not a chicken!' said Jack, exasperated. Why did adults have to make everything so complicated? 'I am not, repeat not, playing a chicken. It's a musical – *Annie Get Your Gun*. How would a chicken get into that?'

'She could be shooting the chicken,' suggested Dad. But then he gave Mum a significant look. 'It doesn't matter what you're playing, does it? The point is you're settling in.'

'Oh, brilliantly!' said Jack sarcastically.

'It takes time,' said Mum contentedly, in the voice she used to praise Frank's achievements.

This annoyed Jack. What did Mum know about the harsh realities of school life? Precious little! He bet no one had tried to stick her head in a dustbin …

'I'm going to take Jasper for a walk,' he said, moodily. He called Jasper and put him on his lead, the lead that had scarcely been used back home. 'I'll be some time,' he warned his parents. Playing a chicken, what were they like!

The traffic was relentless. Wherever he could, Jack crossed at a pedestrian crossing, but these were no guarantee of safety. The rush-hour travellers resented the intrusion of walkers into their world, and more than once Jack and Jasper had to leap on to the pavement. Everyone was focused on getting somewhere else – fast.

They went towards the park that Jack had avoided up to

now because it was the last place he wanted to bump into Ronan's gang. But now he felt all right. Even if Ronan was going to take action, he wouldn't have had time to muster his forces yet, and now that he had seen him running away, Jack was pretty sure that Ronan was too cowardly to act on his own. In fact, he was probably at home right now, crying into his pillow. Jack smiled to himself at the thought of it.

'Hi,' a voice called out from the other side of the park. It was Andrew.

Jack waved back as Andrew came towards him. Only as Andrew leaned forward to check for his mole did he remember that he had forgotten to wash it off!

Jack hoped like crazy that Andrew wouldn't notice. But his luck was out.

Andrew's eyes were drawn to the mole. 'I thought so,' he said. 'You're Jasper, aren't you? I'm in Jack's class at school.'

'Hi.'

'Where's Jack?'

'I think he's still at school – auditions for the school play – or something like that.'

'This your dog?'

Always delighted to receive any attention, Jasper was wagging his tail and panting.

'Is he friendly?'

'Oh, yes,' said Jack, repeating what Mum and Dad always said about him. 'Jasper hasn't got an aggressive bone in his body.' Too late, he remembered that he was

supposed to be Jasper. 'I mean, my dog, that is this dog …'
He trailed off.

Andrew gave him an odd look. 'OK.' He patted Jasper vigorously. 'Tell Jack I've got an idea for our project.'

Jack nodded. Afterwards he wished he'd asked, 'What project?'

'What's his name?' asked Andrew.

Jasper was jumping up and licking his face.

Quick! Emergency brainwave required! 'Em, it's Basil,' gulped Jack, wondering whether he'd ever be able to say anything truthful ever again. At this rate, he'd need a wall chart just to keep track of his own lies.

12

The Project

Ronan, humbled and quiet, or Ronan indignant and determined on revenge? By the next morning Jack could not decide which he was going to encounter at school. Perhaps he won't care that it was Jasper who got at him, Jack said to himself over breakfast. An identical twin brother might get him out of a jam if Ronan snitched to the school – 'What, me, sir? It wasn't me. You remember, I was auditioning for the school play.' But if Ronan used his pals to retaliate, then Jack was in for a hard time. His plan had worked only if 'Jasper' had managed to frighten Ronan off.

He headed off to school, turning each corner cautiously, but his first sighting of Ronan was at assembly. Jack avoided eye contact, so he wasn't sure whether Ronan was looking at him. Still, it looked hopeful. He hadn't got that creepy feeling in his back yet, and there was no insane laughter directed at him – or anyone else. Ronan was remarkably quiet. Was this a good sign?

* * *

'I said, we're the only ones who aren't doing something that's alive,' repeated Andrew.

They were in geography class, and were meant to be working, like everyone else, but Jack was finding it difficult to concentrate and they had met an obstacle. This was annoying, as they had seemed to be ahead of the rest of the class. While others had been debating basics such as whether to make frogs or toads their subject, Jack and Andrew had been racing away with cars, so to speak. There were so many aspects of the subject they wanted to look into. How many cars were there in the city? How many people owned them? What length of journeys did they do, and for what purpose? What speed did they travel at? How many accidents did they have? There were so many questions to ask, it made a project on the natterjack toads look straightforward.

Bunny had ambled over when they had been writing down their ideas, and pointed this out. 'Very impressive,' he had said. 'You're about to undertake the most thorough survey of Dublin traffic ever attempted. A hundred Ministry of Transport officials working flat out wouldn't finish this before 2010. And I want these projects in by next week.'

There were groans from the whole class at this.

'It's a brilliant idea, boys, but you've got to make it workable. How about choosing a specific area?' Bunny had advised. 'And find a theme.'

So now they were stuck, trying to work out how to cut down the topic and give it a single theme.

'We can't even get the info for your topic from books or off the Internet,' complained Andrew. 'We should have chosen elephants or something easy.'

'Yeah,' agreed Jack. 'But this is meant to be about the environment and everyone else is doing animals that aren't even here! At least our project is about where we ...' He stopped, remembering that Andrew had told him last evening in the park that he had an idea. Should he ask him? Would brother Jasper have passed on the message?

'What?' asked Andrew.

'Jasper said something about you having an idea ... something like that. He's not very good at passing on messages.' That had the ring of authenticity.

'Right! My dad was saying how all the roads around here are used for parking. People go into the city to work and leave their cars here 'cos it's free.'

'That's it!' said Jack.

'What's it?'

'It's about where we live – why not do it on Avondale Road?'

'Yeah,' Andrew agreed, 'we could start by counting the cars travelling through.'

'So the first step will be to record the registration numbers of the cars owned by the people who live in the road,' said Jack.

Bunny was over the other side of the room debating

with a dinosaur enthusiast whether dinosaurs counted as part of the environment, and they called him over to tell him what they had decided to do.

'Well done!' he approved. 'I look forward to hearing how you get on.'

Jack and Andrew were pleased, feeling they had accomplished something.

'So, your brother, is he at a special school or something?' asked Andrew gently.

'No!' Too late Jack realised that a twin that was all brawn and no brains might have been useful. He could have used Jasper like a James Bond villain. 'I myself abhor violence, Mr Bond, but my twin brother over there is not so fastidious ...' It was a curious reaction, he realised, to want to defend a brother who did not exist.

'No offence,' said Andrew apologetically. 'It's just that he seemed a bit muddled.'

'That's because he's nearly always thinking about other things,' said Jack. 'Actually, he's brilliant.' A Jack brainwave! 'That's one of the reasons Mum and Dad sent him to a different school, so we wouldn't be made to compete. Some people don't expect you to be individuals. It's like, "Jasper O'Keefe does this, so why don't you?"'

Jack noticed he was actually managing to feel quite resentful at being made to compete with a non-existent twin. He stopped. Alarm bells were ringing. The more he said, the more he had to remember. And this was his new friend, the one person who was prepared to give him a chance.

'So, are you, like, really close? Do you do everything together?'

Now, this was actually difficult to answer truthfully. Getting reacquainted with truth was going to be difficult. Was the honest answer 'Yes, Jasper and I do everything together'? Or was it 'You'll never see us in the same room'? Fortunately, a commotion at the back of the classroom made it easy to avoid both.

'No Brains' Mallet had decided to break up his wooden ruler, stack the pieces and set fire to them. It was not much of a blaze, more smoke than fire, but that is not how Bunny saw it. He swiftly emptied the wastepaper bin, and swept the smouldering ruler into it with his bare hands. The rest of the lesson was devoted to watching 'No Brains' write 'Pyromania is not a sensible career choice' on the blackboard two hundred times, while Bunny talked about the greenhouse effect of carbon gases.

13

Rosalind

Jack headed out of school warily. Any hedge or wall could be concealing Ronan's gang. He forced himself to walk rather than run. He had to look as if he didn't have a care in the world. They'd be on him if he looked scared.

He saw a figure running towards him in a Penrock College jumper and was relieved to recognise Andrew.

'I've got to get some shopping for my gran. Want to come along?' asked Andrew as he reached Jack.

Jack agreed readily. Andrew made him far less vulnerable and anyway, he liked him. He also liked glimpsing the life Andrew led. It was the way Jack imagined it would be if he had a bigger family. There'd always be something happening, thought Jack, someone to hang around with, someone on your side in a fight. He'd quite like an eccentric gran living nearby to look after.

They went to number 62 and collected Gran's shopping list. It had only two items on it but the old lady obviously enjoyed writing it out in her large shaky scrawl.

'Have you seen Rosalind?' she asked as soon as they arrived. She had been waiting in the hall.

'Is she the tortoiseshell cat?' asked Jack, then repeated, 'IS SHE THE TORTOISESHELL CAT?'

The old lady nodded, straining her neck to look at Jack. 'She has a lovely coat.' She was shaking, and Jack realised she was worried about her missing cat. How Basil would manage the city traffic had been his first worry when Dad had told him they were moving to the city. Jasper he was less worried about. You could put a dog on a lead, or keep him in the back garden, but you could not do that with a cat.

'We'll look out for her when we do the shopping,' Andrew promised, signalling to Jack that they should stay for a while to try to stop Gran worrying. They told her about the school day, emphasising the work bits and omitting 'No Brains' Mallet's attempt to burn the school down.

When they told her about the project, she shuffled away. Jack thought she had gone to look for the cat once more, but when she returned she said, 'Here, I've got something for you.' She was carrying an old tin box in her arthritic hands. 'Farrar's Original Harrogate Toffee,' they read on the side of the blue tin.

The toffee was long since eaten. Now, inside the tin were yellowing photographs. 'These'll help you with that project,' said the old lady.

They thanked her and started looking at the

photographs. They had been taken in Avondale Road.

'Look, my house!' said Jack. He could clearly see the number on the front wall.

'All those railings are gone,' remarked Andrew.

'And look at this lot!' Jack held up a photograph of six children playing. They were all girls, dressed in white, with ribbons in their hair.

Gran stretched her neck up to look at the photograph that he held. 'Which one've you got? Oh, that must have been taken on a Sunday. We're in our Sunday best.'

'Sunday best,' repeated Andrew. 'Which one's you, Gran?' Then again, 'WHICH ONE'S YOU?'

Gran pointed to a girl playing with a skipping rope. She was jumping, and her plaited hair was flying up as she did so, while two of her friends held an end of the rope each. They covered the width of the road.

'Wow, no one could do that now, not even on a Sunday!' exclaimed Andrew.

'You'd be dead if you tried!' agreed Jack.

'These are great, Gran! We can use them to show how cars have changed this road.'

'Yes, thanks,' agreed Jack, taking his signal from Andrew to get up to leave.

'Look out for Rosalind,' Gran reminded them. 'She's usually the first in for tea.'

They left her in the tiny front garden of her house. She held a bowl full of dried cat food in her hands and kept calling, 'Rosalind!'

'I hope she doesn't go out searching in the street,' said Andrew, looking nervously back as they turned the corner. 'My kid sister would have more chance in the traffic than Gran would.'

14

The Search

Casually Andrew squeezed between two parked cars and sprinted across the road towards The Korner Shoppe.

Jack followed cautiously. He wanted to be sure none of Ronan's gang was inside before he ventured in. He paused, and, while his eyes scanned the interior, he pointed at the shop sign. 'That would be a really cool name for this shop if it *wasn't* on a corner.'

Andrew laughed. 'Did Jasper think of that?'

The only customers were a woman in a red coat and two little children with her. Jack relaxed a little. 'No, that was definitely me.' He kept wondering if he should tell Andrew how things were between him and Ronan. Andrew had been in the maths class, so he would hardly be surprised.

They bought Gran a loaf of bread and some cheese and bought some chocolate for themselves.

'Better look for Rosalind,' said Andrew, holding the loaf by its wrapper and swinging it round his head.

'Where's she likely to go?' Jack knew that, before they had moved, Basil had had his clearly defined territory and a careful timetable of visits. He guessed that Rosalind would be the same.

Andrew shrugged. 'She usually sticks to the garden, I think. A bit like Gran. Gran hasn't been out by herself for ten years. Rosalind likes sitting by the gate.'

Jack started looking under cars and over walls into gardens. 'She'll probably be somewhere in Avondale Road, then. Once we lost Basil and we found him miles away ...'

'Yeah, but he's a dog, isn't he? They're different.'

Too late Jack remembered that he had said Jasper was Basil when he, that is Jasper, had met Andrew in the park. He hesitated, wondering whether he could claim that both his dog and his cat were called Basil (in order to economise on nametags?).

A change of subject seemed a good idea. 'Why don't we record the registration numbers for our project?' he suggested. 'That way we can catch up and we'll get a chance to search for Rosalind.' He had kept his schoolbag with him, although Andrew had dumped his in Gran's hallway.

'OK,' agreed Andrew. 'Lend us pen and paper.'

They each took a side of the road and noted registration numbers. Even at four-thirty in the afternoon, nearly every parking space was taken.

Jack was wondering where all the people coming home from work were going to park when he heard his mum calling.

Andrew and Jack ran down the road to meet her.

'Jack!' she called out as they approached.

In a moment of dread, Jack realised that if Andrew mentioned Jasper to his mum, the game was up. But the look on her face showed she had something to tell him. She peered forward. 'Jack?'

'Yes, it's me, Jack,' Jack replied, hoping this sounded like a 'Yes, it's me, not Jasper' kind of response. Actually, he realised that Mum wasn't wearing her contact lenses. Without them she was half-blind. When she had taken him swimming, she had made him wear a ridiculous hat just so she could recognise him in the pool.

'Where've you been? I was hoping you'd come straight home when school ended.'

'We were shopping for Andrew's gran. What's wrong?'

'There's been an accident. I saw it, sort of, when I was on the phone to Auntie Pat.'

'What accident?'

'Someone hit something. I heard it and saw someone go into that house.' She pointed to number 60.

'Cuthbert!' said Andrew. 'My gran lives next door.'

'So you're Andrew,' said Mum. 'I've met your gran.'

'Mum, who was hurt? Cuthbert?'

'No, he drove off afterwards. But first he picked something up and took it into his house. And I found this on the road.' Mum was holding part of a numberplate in her hand. It wasn't clear what the number was.

'So you didn't see what he hit?' asked Andrew.

'It might have been a cat,' said Mum. 'I just saw a shape.'

'We're already looking for a cat! Andrew's gran has lost Rosalind.'

'Was it a tortoiseshell cat?' asked Andrew.

'I couldn't tell,' said Mum. 'I just saw a shape. I've got to go and put my lenses in. I don't feel safe with all this traffic.'

The boys ran across the road as Jack's mum made her way cautiously home.

'I'd better check if Rosalind's home,' said Andrew. 'She might have gone in when we were at the shops. You keep looking.'

Jack agreed. He didn't want to see the old lady's face when Andrew told her about the accident, but it meant being out on the streets by himself for a while. Cautiously he crouched down and checked under every parked car. He wasn't worried about being hit by traffic. It was a sudden ambush by Ronan that did worry him.

Eventually, Andrew came out of number 62, shaking his head. 'Rosalind's not back. I told Gran what your mum saw. We've got to ask next door.'

'If Cuthbert did run Rosalind over, he'll be taking her to the vet's, won't he?' asked Jack.

'Don't you believe it! My mum never saw her guinea pigs again when they got into Cuthbert's garden. He's a psycho!'

Reluctantly, they went up the path to number 60. The

gate was off its hinges and propped up against the hedge. Now it was Andrew's turn to look worried. He rang the doorbell and they both stood waiting. All was quiet inside and no one came to answer the bell.

'Supposing it wasn't Rosalind Cuthbert hit?' suggested Jack as they left number 60's front garden. 'Perhaps it was a bit of his gate he took inside.'

'No, I reckon it was Rosalind,' said Andrew disconsolately. 'If she's dead, Cuthbert won't even give Gran back the ...'

He was interrupted by the sound of metal dustbin lids clashing together. Ronan had emerged from the alley by number 32. Colm 'Cock' Roche was behind him. Colm pulled his tie around like a noose and let his tongue hang out. Ronan held the dustbin lids like cymbals.

Just when you thought things couldn't get worse, thought Jack. Mum was upset, Andrew's gran was distressed, and a cat was dead or injured. So, to improve the situation, add Ronan to the scene!

'It's OK,' said Andrew quietly to Jack. 'I know how to handle him.'

Jack still felt his tongue drying out and his back crawling. He watched nervously while Andrew strode up to Ronan. 'OK, Ronan, here's the deal. There's a cat missing and a psycho's probably taken it. Are you going to let him get away with it?'

Jack watched Ronan carefully. If Ronan smirked and said something like, 'Ran over a cat? Nice one!' then Jack was going to land the first blow, relying on Andrew to fight 'Cock' Roche.

But Ronan was interested, despite himself. He said, 'What, that plonker next door to your gran?'

Jack decided to risk talking directly to Ronan and Colm. He had to play it for all it was worth. 'Yeah, he ran over the cat. We don't know if he killed it!' If Rosalind appeared now, meowing for her tea, it would be an end to Gran's problem but his would be far from over.

Ronan flung down the dustbin lids and rushed up the path to number 60. He hammered on the door. Soon Colm joined him. 'Hey Loonie, we know you're in there. Come on out! Where's the cat?' yelled Ronan.

Jack let out his breath. He realised he'd been holding it all the time. It was amazing how Ronan and 'Cock' Roche had homed in on the action. All they needed was something loud and hostile to do. It seemed a pity to burst their bubble by pointing out, 'He's probably not in. Mum saw him drive off.'

'And she saw him run over the cat?' asked 'Cock' Roche.

'She might have. She saw him hit something and pick it up, but she couldn't see too well,' explained Jack, trying not to sound apologetic.

'Great, a blind witness!' complained Ronan.

'But the point is,' said Andrew, 'my gran's cat is definitely missing. So we've got to look for it, OK?'

Jack realised that searching for a cat wasn't in the same league as confronting a psychopathic killer. So, to sweeten the deal, he added, 'And if we don't find her, we'll have to get into number 60 *somehow* and retrieve the body.' Seeing Andrew's face, he added, 'Or rescue her. She could be alive.'

'Why don't we break in right now?' suggested Ronan. 'You said the place is empty.'

'I said Cuthbert's out. Mrs Cuthbert's probably in. She's not allowed to answer the door,' said Andrew.

'And it's broad daylight,' said Jack, as if he had no objection to breaking into a place in the dark.

'OK, so we make sure the cat's not around here,' said Ronan, his tone making it clear that finding Rosalind safe and well was going to be a disappointing end to the enterprise. He and Colm started to look under parked cars.

'Don't you want to know what the cat looks like?' asked Jack. No wonder they thought he was a genius for understanding factors!

Andrew described what Rosalind looked like, then glanced at his watch. 'I hope we find her in the next ten minutes. I've got a dancing lesson soon. I'll have to go!'

Jack waited to hear the mocking laughter from Ronan and Colm at the mention of a dancing lesson, but it did not come. In fact, he noticed something like respect in their manner. Had he misheard? Perhaps Andrew had said he had a trial with Manchester United, and it had just sounded like 'I've got a dancing lesson'. What a fighter Andrew must be, thought Jack. That was the only explanation he could think of for the respect Andrew had.

They went on searching. The name 'Rosalind' was yelled and shouted again and again.

'Don't shout her name so loud!' Andrew called after them. 'Any sane cat would hide from you if she could!'

Ronan and Colm grinned, taking the remark as a compliment, and redoubled their efforts. They overturned dustbins, took down hanging baskets, and walked out in the traffic to check under the roadside wheels of every parked car. Then Ronan suggested searching the back gardens.

Jack thought this was a good idea, but calculated that Ronan would interpret agreement as weakness. He wasn't about to become one of Ronan's yes-men. He kept quiet.

Andrew said, 'OK. Cats get out of traffic as soon as they can. Let's ring on front doors and ask if we can have a look.'

'Yeah, but if they're not in, they won't see us climb over to search,' grinned Ronan.

They started, and five gardens were soon eliminated from their enquiries. Cuthbert's garden seemed impenetrable, having glass and barbed wire on the top of the walls.

Colm was heaved over the wall into five more and reported back that there was no injured cat. 'That one had glass on the top of the wall!' he complained.

'Here, wrap this jumper round your hands, you wuss!' said Ronan unsympathetically, though Jack noticed he wasn't volunteering.

Ronan was loud but a bit of a coward. The way he hadn't fought back when Jack had thrown the eggs showed that. Jack reckoned his reputation was built on noise and conning the most impressionable boys in the class into thinking he had to be obeyed.

'His hands are cut,' Jack pointed out, getting a near-friendly look from Colm. If he could prise his followers away from Ronan, then he'd reduce the threat.

'Go and get some gloves,' Ronan ordered Colm, trying to reassert his authority.

Colm already had torn trousers and a scratch across his face. 'I'm not going all the way home!' he objected.

'I'll get you some gloves,' said Jack, trying to make it sound like a generous offer. It didn't seem to occur to Colm that one of them could do the climbing. He was probably used to taking all the risks. 'In fact, tell you what, I'll take over,' said Jack. 'It won't bother me!'

He was feeling pleased with himself until Andrew spoke. 'Why don't you get Jasper out here?' he suggested.

Jack jolted. He was pretty sure he could find some gloves, but where was he going to find a twin brother?

15

Knocking at
Cuthbert's Door

Jack didn't answer Andrew's suggestion that Jasper should come out as well to help look for Rosalind. He just ran towards home, trying to look as if he was on a mission.

'Did you find her?' Mum shouted to him from the kitchen as he entered the house.

'Not yet! Just came back for some gloves!' Jack shouted back as he leapt up the stairs. When he reached his room, he sat down on the bed to think. If Jasper failed to appear, then Ronan would interpret that as being scared. He could say Jasper wasn't home from school yet. But, with Colm to back him, Ronan might appear at the door of number 13 to check.

Time for a Jack brainwave. He couldn't let Ronan think Jasper was afraid to meet him. Jasper would have to show.

He pulled off his jumper, changed his trousers, put on his St Michael's blazer and drew on the mole. He crept down the stairs and slipped out of the house before Mum could see him, muttering to himself. He was ready with a line for Ronan. 'Want some more of the same, you idiot?'

He crossed the road and resisted slowing down as he ran towards number 60. If Ronan thought he was reluctant to get to him, he'd think he was scared. But when Jack could see up the street, he realised Ronan and Colm were nowhere to be seen. Andrew was on his own.

Jack greeted him as if he hadn't seen him a few minutes before. He was longing to ask what had happened to Ronan and his sidekick, but he reckoned this would be an odd first question for Jasper.

Andrew looked fed up and asked, 'Where's Jack? Has he given up?'

'Course not,' said Jack, not wanting to disappoint Andrew. 'He's just … searching for some gloves or something. You on your own?'

'I am now!' said Andrew indignantly. 'Two boys in my class were here but they scarpered.'

Jack had to struggle not to smile with satisfaction. More evidence that Ronan was, at heart, a coward! He hadn't wanted to encounter Jasper. But Andrew was looking worried and now he thought Jack had abandoned him too.

'Jack's going to help you find the cat,' he assured him. 'I'll go and see what's keeping him.' He ran back to his house and up the stairs, tearing off his St Michael's blazer as he went. He had changed back into his jumper and Penrock College trousers when he heard Mum climbing the stairs.

'What do you need gloves for?' she asked as she got to the top of the stairs.

'Looking under hedges and stuff,' answered Jack, realising she would not be happy that they were climbing into neighbours' gardens.

She sighed. 'I wish I'd had my lenses in! But the more I think about it the surer I am that what I saw was a cat in Mr Cuthbert's arms!'

'He's not in, and, anyway, he's a difficult customer. That's what Andrew's gran says. He might have killed the cat by now!'

'Surely not! As soon as Frank arrives I'll … What are you doing with my eyebrow pencil?'

Jack had left the eyebrow pencil on his bedroom table.

'Em, looking for something to write with.'

His pencil case was on the table too and he waited for Mum to comment, but all she said was, 'That won't work,' and picked it up. 'And gloves are in the bottom drawer.'

Got away with it that time! said Jack to himself as he ran out again and down the road.

Andrew was standing alone outside number 60.

'Thought you had a lesson or something,' said Jack.

'I've missed it now. But guess what?' said Andrew impatiently.

'What?'

'Cuthbert's back! I heard his voice through the wall

when I went into Gran's. He must have come home while I was searching a back garden!'

They stared at each other, both reluctant to venture on to Cuthbert's property.

This was the sort of moment, Jack thought, where Ronan was useful. He'd be hammering on that door and yelling, ''Scuse me, have you seen a cat?' within a second.

But twin Jasper would be just as bold, thought Jack. He couldn't go home and draw on a mole but he'd managed a fearsome performance in front of Ronan. Perhaps he could manage it again. 'I'll ask him,' he said.

'Will you?' asked Andrew, clearly relieved. 'He hates all my family, so don't tell him it's Gran's cat that's missing.'

Jack strode up the pathway and rang the doorbell. He put his finger firmly on the button but not for too long. He didn't want to antagonise Cuthbert. Perhaps he would be reasonable. Perhaps he had taken Rosalind to the vet's and would appear at the door, smiling, with Rosalind in his arms.

Jack's optimism was short-lived. The acrid smell of alcohol hit him as soon as the door opened.

A large red-faced man was standing at the door and leaning back. 'What?' he barked.

'Excuse me, but we're looking for a cat,' stammered Jack. It wasn't Jasper in egg-throwing mode, but at least he managed to get the words out.

'What the hell's that got to do with me?' was the answer he got.

'My mum …' Jack realised that he didn't want Cuthbert getting at his mum. 'I mean, someone saw you, thought they saw you pick up a cat,' said Jack.

'Cats! Filthy animals! Shouldn't be allowed in the city!'

Jack hesitated. He wanted to tell this unpleasant specimen that his sort should be banned, not cats! Cats were intelligent, good-looking and affectionate, and he obviously failed on all three counts! But saying that wouldn't find Rosalind, so instead he began to say, 'But the owner is very …'

Cuthbert interrupted with, 'Come on, come on, this isn't a debating club! Get out of here. And shut the gate!' With that, he slammed the door.

'What's his problem?' muttered Jack, glad to see that Ronan hadn't reappeared. 'And I *can't* shut the gate, it's off its hinges!'

'Told you he'd be like that,' said Andrew. 'When my granddad was dying, Cuthbert complained about the ambulance being parked outside his house!'

They searched along the street again, but soon Jack knew it was time to go. Reluctantly, the boys went their separate ways.

Jack was pinning his hopes on Frank thinking of something. It was already getting dark and within an hour, every cat in Dublin would be invisible.

16

Jack Confuses Himself

When Jack got inside he discovered that Frank had already arrived and Mum had told him and Dad about the accident and the missing cat. They were sitting at the kitchen table eating and discussing whether Rosalind had been hit by the car.

Dad had been forced to buy fish and chips from the chippy because the eggs Mum had planned to make into omelettes had mysteriously disappeared. Jack managed to look baffled when they told him this but he couldn't help casting a glance at Frank. It was difficult to kid a kidder, but Frank seemed to be more interested in whether there was a connection between the accident his aunt had heard and the disappearance of the cat.

Jack told them all about his encounter with Cuthbert, stressing his rudeness and dislike of cats – a capital crime in his family. They were all bristling with indignation by the time he had finished.

'Trouble is,' Frank complained, 'cats don't count for much under the law. It's not even an offence to run over a cat under the Road Traffic Act. The motorist doesn't have to stop.'

'That can't be right,' said Dad indignantly.

Frank shrugged. 'It's just one of those anomalies in the law.'

'What's an anomaly?' Jack asked between gulps of fish and chips. He was putting one chip in his mouth and the next in Jasper's.

'It means it doesn't add up. You take a chocolate bar from a shop and you're a criminal. Deliberately run over a cat and you're OK!'

There and then Jack decided to become a lawyer just to change that law. But, in a shorter time-scale, something had to be done about finding Rosalind!

The doorbell rang. Jack went to answer it, followed, as always, by Jasper.

Andrew stood in the porch. He leaned forward, scrutinised Jack's face and asked, 'Jasper? Jack?'

Jasper leapt up affectionately at Andrew on hearing his name and Jack's hand flew to his right cheek. Had he drawn on the mole? Yes! Had he scrubbed it off? He couldn't remember doing it before rushing out to help Andrew search for Rosalind again. He wanted to look in the hall mirror to check, but knew that would be a dead giveaway. You don't have to look in a mirror to check if you've got a mole when you've had one all your life. Then he realised he was wearing a Penrock College jumper. That made him Jack!

Fortunately, patting Jasper had distracted Andrew from his own question and he had some news he was desperate to impart. 'I've found Rosalind! At least I think I have!'

Frank heard and came into the hallway. 'This Andrew?' he asked.

Jack nodded, realising he would have to invite Andrew in and hope he could tell his story without mentioning twins, and that the family wouldn't introduce their pets as they usually did.

He cast one quick look at the mirror before leading Andrew into the kitchen. Yes, he still had the mole! That made him either Jasper dressed in Jack's school uniform or Jack who had inexplicably grown a mole. Neither seemed likely and he leaned against the kitchen wall trying to work out what he was going to say to them all if Andrew asked him again which twin he was.

However, Andrew was intent on his account of what had happened when he had gone into his gran's house. He had realised that he could get a good view of most of Cuthbert's garden and the conservatory built on the back of the house if he went upstairs and leaned out the window of the boxroom. He had done this and seen a shape in Cuthbert's conservatory that he was sure was Rosalind.

Dad, Mum and Frank questioned him and were soon convinced he had seen the missing cat. He described her as lying still but not as if she were dead. They discussed what should be done. Jack tried to join in just enough to stop someone asking, 'And what do you think, Jack?' and not so much that anyone would say, 'That point Jack just made was a good one.'

Eventually, after they had agreed that approaching Cuthbert directly and appealing to his better nature would be futile (Andrew had convinced them that Cuthbert didn't have one), and that a check should be kept on Rosalind until they could formulate a plan, Jack found a moment to rush upstairs, wash off the mole and change into T-shirt and jeans. He came downstairs to hear Frank was borrowing Dad's car and Andrew was going back to keep an eye on Rosalind. If he could just follow Andrew out of the house, he would have got through the whole encounter without twins being mentioned.

He nearly made it until Andrew asked, 'Can Jack and Jasper come round to number 62?'

Mum and Dad stared.

'Jack can,' Mum answered, 'but Jasper better stay here.'

Dad added, 'Jasper's not keen on cats. He likes to chase them!'

Now it was Andrew's turn to stare, but Jack bundled him out of the house quickly, saying, 'Come on! We'd better check Cuthbert's not up to anything!'

17

Saving Rosalind

Frank followed after them. He pulled Jack aside and asked quietly, 'You OK?'

Jack was tempted to confide in Frank. His cousin was the only person he knew in the world to whom he could say, 'It's just that I'm pretending to be two people at once. I've got an identical twin, right?'

Knowing Frankie, he'd probably reply, 'Oh, the identical twin ploy? Used it myself on numerous occasions!'

But, with Andrew standing waiting, all Jack could do was nod and ask, 'Are you coming back?'

'Sure am! Now listen, Jack. This is very important. You know my mobile number? Call me right away if this cat is not in the conservatory of ...' Frank looked at the house. 'Of number 60. OK?'

He dashed off and Jack and Andrew went into number 62.

They found Gran looking hunched and thinner, like an ill-fed bird of prey. Worry had drained life from her and she went to her bedroom to try to sleep.

The boys went to the boxroom, and Jack leaned out of the window to get a view of Cuthbert's conservatory. He could see a still curled shape that could be Rosalind. They stayed, leaning out of the window every few minutes to check that the neighbour from hell hadn't entered the conservatory.

They kept quiet for a while. Jack was dreading Andrew saying something about Jasper. How had he got into this situation?

If it wasn't for the twin thing, life in Dublin was improving. He was getting used to the streets and the traffic and he had a friend at Penrock now. He'd put Ronan to flight once and was chipping away at his Evil Empire.

If only he hadn't told Andrew about having a twin brother too! He could hardly expect a friend to call for him at home and not work out that he didn't have a brother. Still, here he was helping Andrew with his gran's problem and contributing the mighty powers of Frank to the enterprise. So, if it worked OK, Andrew should be grateful. *And*, if he did something that would impress Ronan and Co., so much the better.

'We need something to throw at Cuthbert if he makes a move towards Rosalind,' said Jack.

Andrew went away and returned with a stack of milk bottles.

'Fortunately, the milkman *does* still call here!' he said.

Lights shone from the houses backing onto the alley and

occasionally a dog barked in a distant garden. There was no sound from next door, although the kitchen light was on, casting a glow on the garden. Rosalind was a small, still shape in the conservatory.

'Did Frankie say call him if she was there, or if she wasn't?' asked Andrew as they waited.

'If she wasn't. Do you think Cuthbert'll kill her?' Jack whispered.

'Yes.'

Finally, faintly, from the front of the houses, they heard the sound of a doorbell. They went into a front bedroom to check. Gently, Andrew pulled back the curtains and they looked down.

Someone had called at the house next door. He, and it was a he, judging by the deep voice they heard and the flat cap they could see, was talking to someone at the door. They could not see the figure, but they heard Mrs Cuthbert's fluttery tones. She closed the door on him. He looked up.

'It's Frank!' hissed Jack.

Frank was gesturing to the alleyway.

'He wants us to go down to the garden, I think,' said Andrew.

Frank had gone, but Cuthbert had charged out of the front door like a bull. The boys heard him roaring with anger as they ran down the stairs towards the back door.

Andrew unlocked and unbolted the back door and they rushed out. Jack started to jump up to see over the fence and barbed wire. He saw nothing, but he heard a clicking sound. 'I think Frank's cutting through the barbed wire!' he whispered to Andrew.

'Suppose Cuthbert comes round? Where's Mrs Cuthbert? She'll tell him if she sees Frank!' Even cool Andrew was starting to panic.

Jack needed some of his brainwaves right now. 'Try to keep Cuthbert round the front! I'll stay here to help Frank and create a diversion if I have to!'

Andrew ran into the house.

'Frank, what's happening?' Jack whispered over the fence. There was no answer, but he thought he heard a rustling noise in next door's garden and Frank whispering gently. Should he go to help Andrew? Or should he wait for Frankie?

He was about to run through the house to check on Andrew when he heard the smashing of glass. He waited, looking around to see if there was anything in the garden he could use to climb on. He had to see what was happening at number 60!

'Jack? Grab her!'

Jack overturned a dustbin and leapt onto it. A pair of thickly gloved hands appeared over the fence. He reached up, just in time to catch Rosalind as Frank dropped her over the fence.

Jack ran into the house and laid Rosalind down as gently as he could. His heart was racing. He wanted to lock the back door straight away. Where had Frank gone? And where was Andrew?

He ran to the front of the house to find Andrew rushing in.

'Keep quiet!' ordered Andrew, switching off the light in the hall.

They crept into the unlighted sitting room and stared through the grimy net curtains. Cuthbert was angrily kicking his own car!

'What's he doing?' whispered Jack.

'He's going berserk, that's what. His car's been clamped!'

Jack could just see the yellow metal gripping the front wheel of Cuthbert's car. He was throwing his weight behind every kick he gave it. Then, Jack and Andrew heard a familiar voice: 'Serves you right, you eejit!'

Cuthbert turned to look across the road. 'D'you do this?' he demanded.

'Ronan!' exclaimed Jack.

Ronan, flanked by Colm and 'No Brains', was baiting Cuthbert from a safe distance.

'Did Ronan get Cuthbert's car clamped?' questioned Andrew incredulously.

'No!' said Jack emphatically. Ronan being that smart was some scary thought! 'He must have turned up to see what we were doing about Cuthbert,' said Jack. He knew who would have the contacts and the know-how to organise a clamping. His cousin had had some interesting vacation jobs.

Cuthbert's angry face was turned to Ronan's gang. They

hadn't done a thing to him, but they were happy to take the credit. An inspired insult from Brian sent Cuthbert lurching across the road. The boys turned and ran, with Cuthbert in pursuit.

'Let's get Rosalind to my place while we can,' said Jack.

'Shouldn't we wake Gran?'

'Wait'll we see what Mum and Dad say first,' said Jack. He thought Rosalind looked very sick. She hadn't moved from the kitchen where he'd lain her. 'There's no point worrying her.'

They took the injured Rosalind across to number 13.

As soon as they saw the state of Rosalind, Jack's mum drove to the nearest vet's with a twenty-four hour emergency service. Rosalind's hips had been dislocated and she was kept in the animal hospital for observation, as there were possible complications. However, the vet said that the most likely thing would be that Rosalind would have to be confined to one room for a month to allow the injury to heal. Gran was woken and told the news. She was happy that Rosalind was alive and no longer held by Cuthbert.

On returning from the vet's, there was a mood of euphoria in the kitchen of number 13. Everyone was relieved at Rosalind's rescue and the fact that her injuries were not life-threatening.

'Basil had the same thing once,' Mum recalled. 'It's quite common, especially in cats.'

'But it must be a lot harder to keep a dog in a room for a month,' said Andrew.

Oh, no, thought Jack. Twin alert.

'Er ... so Cuthbert came out and found his car clamped!' Jack said, changing the subject. He did not have to ask who was responsible, but he wondered if it had occurred to Mum and Dad.

'Yes, I just don't understand that!' said Mum, laughing happily. 'I thought that was something that only happened if people parked in private car parks or something, not outside their own house.'

'It usually is,' explained Dad. 'The wheel clamp hasn't got any marking on it. Frank used to work for a wheel-clamping company before he was qualified, so he'd know who to contact, but we aren't going to help that scoundrel! Cuthbert'll have to have his car towed to a garage and have the whole wheel taken off!'

Sometimes it's useful having parents who live in a world of their own, thought Jack. He began to say something quickly just in case they started to put the pieces of the puzzle together, but Andrew went one better. He went into acting mode and imitated Cuthbert. 'He was really red in the face, and kicking his own car! I thought he would have a heart attack!'

'Well, it's his wife I feel sorry for,' said Mum, after she had laughed heartily at Andrew's impression.

Then she decided she'd better adopt a more responsible tone. 'Now, you boys have got school in the morning, don't forget. Time to get to bed.' She looked at Andrew. 'Do you want to go back to your gran's? You can stay here if you like.'

'Is that OK?' asked Andrew.

'Won't your gran want you back?' asked Jack desperately. He felt far too tired even to try to be twin Jasper as well as twin Jack.

Andrew shook his head. 'Gran's already asleep. I don't want to disturb her again.'

'So that's settled,' said Dad. 'You can sleep on the bottom bunk. Jack always sleeps on the top bunk and Jasper usually sleeps on the bottom one, but he can resume his rightful place for one night.'

Jack looked quickly at Andrew to see how he would take this. He just nodded.

Mum turned the stair light on. 'Up you go!'

Though tired, Jack tried to think quickly. If he could retrieve Mum's eyebrow pencil, he would be able to draw on his mole. He could wander into his bedroom, say something like, 'Hi! So what's been happening?' and listen, then go out, scrub off the mole, come back as Jack ...

He realised he didn't have the energy! As he slowly climbed the stairs, Jack made a decision: Jasper would have to be disposed of. He had outlived his usefulness. Should he meet his death in a freak boating accident, perhaps? The trouble was Mum and Dad would be expected to be in mourning, and they clearly weren't. He could hear them chatting away happily downstairs.

When all else fails, try the truth. As they reached the top of the stairs, Jack turned to Andrew and said, 'There's just one other thing ...'

18

Rat Running

'About Jasper ...'

'Yeah?'

'He's my dog.'

'So that's why there's a dog bowl in your kitchen with *Jasper* on it!' Andrew was smiling.

Jack felt relieved that Andrew was prepared to take the whole thing as a joke, but the next words were painful nevertheless. 'I haven't got a brother. There's just me.'

Just me had often seemed like a very short sentence. Even times like opening Christmas presents were lonely when there was no one to share it with you.

'I started to figure that out when you opened the front door and I saw a mole on your cheek.'

'It was the only way I could get Ronan off my back!' Jack told Andrew about his egg ambush.

Andrew laughed. 'So that's why he ran when he thought Jasper was on his way! Don't worry about Ronan.

I can have him eating out of my hand.'

'How come?'

'Because I'm on telly a lot. Dancing.'

'Wow!'

Jack was relieved he had come clean with Andrew. Whether it was because of that or helping rescue Rosalind, he slept soundly. He didn't wake in the morning until Jasper bounded up the stairs and leapt onto the bottom bunk, and Andrew yelled out as he wrestled with the golden retriever.

Mum put her head round the door. 'No time to play with the dog now,' she said, as if Andrew had chosen to have thirty kilos covered in fur land on him. 'You'll be late for school if you don't both get up right now!'

'I've phoned the vet. Rosalind had a comfortable night,' Dad told them as they came into the kitchen. 'If you hop in the car right now, I'll drop you at school. You might get there before the bell rings.'

Jack heard the phone just as they were leaving the house. It was Frank. 'You OK?' his cousin asked him.

'Fine! Thanks for everything, Frankie!'

'A pleasure, kid. You didn't elaborate on my part in the proceedings?'

'No!'

'That waster got what he deserved. I'm not the only one to think so. Mrs Cuthbert gave me the cat!'

'What?'

'Yeah, she handed me Rosalind through the conservatory doors.'

'But I heard glass smashing,' objected Jack.

'I did that so Cuthbert wouldn't realise his wife helped me,' explained Frank. 'There's one odd thing, though ...'

'What's that?'

Dad was beeping his horn and Mum was tapping at her watch to tell Jack he was late for school.

'Cuthbert's car didn't have a scratch on it. And both numberplates were firmly attached!'

Jack had to put the phone down, but his mind was spinning with the implications of what Frank had told him. How had Cuthbert managed to knock his own gate off its hinges and run over Rosalind without putting a scratch on his car? Had they got the wrong man? If he hadn't run over Rosalind, why had he taken her prisoner?

Jack ran to the car, and Dad drove away even before Jack had managed to pull the back door shut. The car sped along, but there was time, as they passed Cuthbert's, to see that the wheel clamp was still firmly in place and that, as Frankie had told him, the car was undamaged.

Dad came to a halt on the double yellow lines outside the school just as the bell was sounding.

'Geography second lesson,' Andrew called back as they raced towards their classroom. 'Let's say our theme is rat running. Yes?'

Ronan, Colm 'Cock' Roche and 'No Brains' surrounded them, wanting to know if the cat had been retrieved from Cuthbert's.

'Yep, we got her!' said Jack, and told them how, but

with Frank edited out of the story. Now, in the retelling, he and Andrew wheel-clamped Cuthbert's car, used the wire-cutters and broke into Cuthbert's conservatory.

Andrew went along with the tale and Jack could see their prestige growing. It certainly made the gang's dustbin ploy sound lame!

'Wow,' said 'Cock' Roche, unable to conceal his admiration. 'You know how to get a wheel clamp put on?'

'Sure,' Jack assured him. 'No one messes with our pets!'

He could almost feel Colm being prised away from his one-time mighty leader!

'By the way, what car does *your* dad drive?' he asked Ronan. He got a scowl in reply, but 'Cock' Roche and 'No Brains' grinned.

Putty in my hands, thought Jack with satisfaction.

Unfortunately teachers weren't so malleable. Something had clearly upset Bunny. When, during geography, Jack's thoughts drifted to the Cuthbert situation, he found Bunny snapping at him, 'Jack! Jack! For the third time I am asking you to say what theme you have chosen for your project! Where is your concentration this morning, boy?'

'It's going to be on rat running,' Jack managed. Tiredness was overcoming him. Four hours' sleep was not enough.

Bunny knitted his fingers together, cracked his knuckles, and said sarcastically, 'That is what Andrew told us some five minutes ago. What I am now asking for is a definition of that term!'

Confusion made Jack feel reckless. He had coped with the move. He had kept quiet about the bullying. He had helped break into a house and rescue a cat. What was next? He gritted his teeth and said, 'Rats are small rodents. There must be a lot about here! Or maybe we should be studying chickens ... and their eggs!'

At the mention of eggs, Ronan looked like someone had poked him in the backside, but he recovered himself and scowled at Jack.

The exchange wasn't lost on Bunny, who gave Jack a curious look and raised an eyebrow.

Jack decided he had gone far enough and he corrected himself. 'I mean it's cars using little roads as shortcuts.' He sighed; the effort was almost too much. 'Residential roads, lots of speeding cars.'

Bunny gave him another penetrating look, then moved on. 'Thank you. Now let us hear from you, Brian. Your project is on the contents of the River Liffey, isn't it?'

'Sick bags all round!' shouted 'No Brains' cheerfully.

Every member of the class had to explain their project and, if he had not felt so tired, Jack would have been pleased by the originality of rat running. As it was, he could hardly keep his eyes open. Was it this that made Bunny seem irritable and troubled? He snapped at them and made sarcastic remarks and by the end of the lesson, the whole class seemed subdued.

But something had revived Ronan. At breaktime, he revealed what it was. Jack and Andrew were leaning on the outside wall, half-sleeping, when Ronan came up and announced, 'Here, Andy, it wasn't that creep next door who ran over your gran's cat. I know who it was!'

This was enough to wake them up.

'Who?' Andrew and Jack asked together, as Colm and 'No Brains' moved in towards them.

'Bunny!'

Andrew stood up. 'Mr Abbott? Don't be a moron!'

Ronan went bright red.

'Oh, I'm a moron, am I? Just because I don't dance about on TV! Come and have a look at this, then!' Ronan jerked his finger towards the school car park. They followed him.

Bunny's car was parked nose-first. Ronan led them to the front of the car. 'Look at that!'

The front numberplate was missing and one wing was damaged! 'I was just looking out the window in geography and I saw it!' declared Ronan with relish.

Absolute disbelief filled Jack, but the evidence was there. He bent down to the car. He could even see some of the blue paintwork from Cuthbert's gate.

'Why should he drive down Avondale Road?' asked Andrew. 'He lives in the opposite direction.'

'But he was real weird this morning,' chipped in 'No Brains'.

Jack was thinking about what Frankie had told him. If he told this lot now, they'd be convinced Bunny was guilty.

'My mum saw Cuthbert reverse his car and hit the cat!' he objected.

'You said she couldn't see very well,' pointed out Ronan.

He was right. Mum without her contact lenses was an unreliable witness. She had seen an accident. Perhaps Cuthbert, in his drunken way, had been trying to help. Bunny had hit the cat, and run into the gate. Cuthbert heard the noise, ran out and picked up the cat, perhaps even meaning to take it to the vet's.

Jack looked around him. Andrew looked dejected. Ronan, 'No Brains' and Colm looked like a lynching party.

19

Cuthbert Looks Innocent

'Anyway,' asked Ronan impatiently, 'what're we going to do about Bunny running over your gran's cat?'

'And not stopping,' added 'No Brains'.

'We could report him to the police!' suggested Colm. 'Then they'd arrest him. Serve him right for giving us so much homework!'

'There's no law against running over cats,' Jack told them. 'It's an anomaly.'

'What's that?' asked 'No Brains', while Ronan roughly flicked the wing mirrors on their hinges.

'It means that someone who doesn't think much of cats made the law,' Jack explained.

'Bunny's still a killer!' declared Ronan with relish. 'Whoops!' he said dramatically. He had broken off the wing mirror on the teacher's car.

Clearly, if Bunny was guilty, he could wave goodbye to a car with four wheels and gleaming paintwork.

Ronan was already planning his moves. 'Hey, where'd you get that wheel clamp from?' he asked Jack and Andrew.

'Hang on,' objected Andrew. 'We don't know he did it. Just because he's lost a numberplate! He could have lost that anytime.'

Break was over, but by the end of the school day news of how Mr Abbott had run over a cat in Avondale Road had spread through the class and beyond. As it spread, it was reported as if Mr Abbott had definitely done it and done it deliberately.

'Well, I don't think he did,' said Andrew as he and Jack walked towards Avondale Road after school. 'I still think it was Cuthbert.'

'But how come his numberplate isn't gone?' asked Jack.

Helping to break into someone's conservatory when they'd run over a cat and hidden it was one thing. It had occurred to Jack that if Cuthbert was just a harmless drunk, then he was going to be furious about the break-in into the conservatory. Jack was dreading seeing a police car outside number 60. If Cuthbert had reported the break-in to the police, then saving Frankie's skin was his priority. He was pretty sure there'd be a rule about lawyers not being burglars …

But there was no police car outside Cuthbert's house. His car was being loaded onto a breakdown vehicle with the clamp still in place. A moment of triumph if he was guilty, but that was looking more unlikely.

Rosalind had been brought back from the vet's and

Gran took them up to the boxroom to see the injured cat. Rosalind was moving in an odd way; her rear limbs scarcely seemed attached to her front. But Gran was up-beat. 'You'll soon be chasing birds again, won't you, my darling?' she cooed.

It would have been a good moment seeing the old lady reunited with her cat, but Jack couldn't stop worrying about whether Cuthbert was innocent and Bunny guilty. Even apart from the repercussions from the break-in, Jack had the feeling that this turn of events shifted the balance of power back to Ronan. They'd told the gang that they had done the wheel-clamping and the break-in, so that could be used against them and, if Ronan used his usual strong-arm tactics on Bunny, he'd have Colm and 'No Brains' on his case again!

An awful thought occurred to Jack. He started to rummage in his schoolbag.

'What is it?' asked Andrew.

Jack was sifting through bits of paper. 'When Rosalind went missing, we were taking down all the numbers of the cars parked in Avondale Road, right?'

'Right!'

'And Mum said the car drove off, so if Cuthbert did it, we won't have his number. Yes?'

Jack was holding the piece of paper he had been looking for in his hand.

'Yes. Do you remember Cuthbert's number?'

'It was something like …'

Jack ran his eyes down the list and, flatly, read out a number.

'That's it,' said Andrew, disappointed too. 'Cuthbert was parked here when we started looking for Rosalind. He didn't run over her! He's innocent!'

20

Twins Again

When Jack and Andrew parted that evening, they hadn't worked out what they should do about their discovery. Jack thought about phoning Frankie. He would have to tell him that it looked as if Cuthbert was innocent of running over Rosalind and that Mr Abbott, his teacher, was guilty. But he decided to keep Frankie out of it if he could. If Cuthbert had complained to the police about the break-in, then the less that Frankie was about the better. Also – and this seemed a disloyal thought, but Jack thought it anyway – he wasn't sure if he wanted any more of Frankie's input.

Frankie's solutions to problems were starting to look like problems in themselves. Jack would never have broken in to the conservatory by himself and he wouldn't have known how to get a car wheel-clamped! Those were Frankie-type solutions. What could he come up with on his own?

Jack lay on his bunk with Jasper snoring beneath him, trying to figure out a way of discovering whether Mr Abbott was guilty. By the morning he'd come up with a Jack brainwave. If it worked, it would help in his battle with Ronan too.

He found Andrew waiting for him at the school gates. 'Ronny's been telling everyone that Bunny tried to kill my gran's cat!' he complained. 'If Bunny gets to hear about it, I bet it'll be me in trouble!'

'I think I know how we can find out,' Jack told him.

'How?'

'We did this play at my old school, called *Hamlet* ...'

'Yeah?'

'In it, Hamlet gets to work out if someone's guilty, by putting on a play where the same thing happens. So what we have to do is incorporate the story of what happened to Rosalind in our project on rat running.'

'See if he goes red and gets angry, you mean?' asked Andrew.

'Yes.'

'But we'll be doing our presentation. Suppose we miss his reaction? Unless he goes crazy or something, we might be too busy reading our notes to see how he reacts.'

'We'll tell everyone. Then they'll all be looking.'

'OK. Let's tell them. But hang on. I've been thinking too.'

'Yes?' said Jack, expecting to hear an addition to his own plan.

Instead he heard Andrew say, 'I think Jasper should make one more appearance!'

'What? Haven't we got enough to think about?'

'No, but listen. Ronny and his lot aren't going to forget about Jasper. They might try to keep out of his way, but if he just disappears even "No Brains" could work out something's fishy!'

'So I've got to make Jasper turn up from now until I leave school?'

'No! Have him turn up, then show it's you and the laugh's on Ronny!'

Jack realised Andrew meant that Jasper should present the project!

'Hang on,' he objected. 'I've got this project, and then after school I've got to go and rehearse being a rooster, or something, in a play about a girl with a gun! I don't need any more pressure.'

'But it's the perfect opportunity to play the joke on Ronny. He'll be gobsmacked if he thinks Jasper has the nerve to come into Jack's school. Then, we don't say anything in school, but afterwards, we tell them all that there is no twin brother and that they're a bunch of gullible idiots for believing there was.'

He sounded convincing. Jack thought about it. It would be a way of turning the tables on Ronan, who was bound to find out about Jasper sometime. And, though he wouldn't be able to wear the blazer, he could draw on the mole and somehow, inexplicably, he felt braver then. He'd need that bravery when challenging Bunny. 'OK, I'll do it.'

Jack thought about it as they went in to class. Twin Jasper

had been for Ronan's benefit, so making out it had been an elaborate practical joke might work. He didn't relish the idea of trying to:

A test his teacher, and

B present his project while

C pretending to be someone he wasn't!

But the biggest problem of all was going to be selling the plan to the gang. Jack knew Ronan would favour something thuggish that he could be in charge of. This plan put him and Andrew in the centre of things. Ronan wouldn't like it, and things that Ronan didn't like usually didn't happen.

The mood against Bunny was growing poisonous. The legend was growing of Bunny, gifted teacher by day, psychotic killer when the school day ended.

At break, as most of the class stood on the edge of the teachers' car park, Andrew began to explain how he and Jack had a way to find out if the teacher was guilty. Just getting some of them to understand what they had planned was tough enough.

'What d'yer mean: "where the same thing happens"?' asked 'No Brains' belligerently, when Jack mentioned *Hamlet*. He used the same tone in maths lessons, in English lessons, in French lessons, in fact every time that he was in danger of not understanding, which was pretty much all the time.

Jack was tempted to ask sarcastically, 'Have you heard of Shakespeare?' but he wanted 'No Brains' on his side, so he patiently explained again how they were going to refer to the events in Avondale Road and watch Bunny's reaction.

When he'd finished, Ronan objected by saying, 'We can't put on a play!' and Jack knew he was misunderstanding on purpose.

The moment was drawing near when he'd have to challenge Ronan directly in front of everyone. It would be make- or break-time. He might end up face-down in a dustbin after all.

'Why don't we just let down the tyres on his car, for starters?' said Ronan, seizing the advantage.

'*Egg*sactly,' replied Jack sarcastically. 'Just what I'd expect from you, Ronny! Who are you named after – Ronnie Kray or that Great Train Robber?'

He addressed the rest of the class. 'If you want to do this properly, you've got to do it the smart way. We can't take action against someone before we know they're guilty.'

He stopped. He couldn't help remembering that that was just what he had done with Cuthbert, but now wasn't the time to mention the fact. He had to seize this moment to get his plan chosen over Ronan's.

'So what are you going for?' he asked. 'Our plan, Plan A – the subtle approach, which won't get us all into trouble if Bunny's innocent – or Plan B, with B standing for *brute force and ignorance*.' Jack waved a hand in Ronan's direction as he said this, and all Ronan's past victims smirked.

'So hands up if you're in favour of Plan A,' said Andrew.

A majority of hands went up but Ronan, Colm and 'No

Brains' kept theirs down. Then, slowly, Colm raised his hand and 'No Brains' did too.

'Right, that's settled then,' said Jack, ignoring Ronan. 'Carried unanimously!'

He was tempted to move away and ignore Ronan, but he knew he should face him at his weakest. 'How about you then, Ronny?' he asked. 'You going to spoil our plan?'

Ronan looked about him for support. There was none. He shrugged. 'I thought of something like that, anyway,' he protested sulkily.

'Of course you did,' laughed Andrew, and the class laughed with him.

21

The Presentation

'Do cars dominate our environment? Are we forced to give way to these monsters instead of them giving way to us? Should we have to put up with this? Shouldn't we control the machines instead of the machines controlling us?'

'Yes, yes, no and yes.'

Andrew and Jack were standing in front of the class. Most of the class thought they were watching Andrew and the new boy give a presentation.

Ronan, Colm and 'No Brains' thought they were watching Andrew and Jack's twin brother, Jasper.

Andrew had let them know before school began that Jasper was taking Jack's place that day at school. He'd left it to the last minute so they couldn't ask too many questions.

Ronan had looked uneasy, then doubtful. 'Give over! Why would they do that?'

'They often do it,' Andrew had said. 'Identical twins do that sort of thing. For a laugh, usually. Of course,' he added, 'it takes a lot of guts.'

When Jack had turned up, he had the mole in place and a scowl on his face. He gave his planned greeting to Colm. 'Oh, it's you from the tobacconist's!' he sneered. He ignored 'No Brains' and narrowed his eyes at Ronan.

'If Jack's got to go to your school, what's the point?' asked Ronan.

'Jack's at home, playing his PlayStation!' Andrew informed him. 'It's a religious holiday. Jasper goes to a religious school so he's got the day off.'

'What religious holiday?' asked Colm.

'The Feast of the Holy Suffragette,' said Jack promptly.

'Why didn't they send Jack to the religious school, then?' asked Colm.

'Well,' snorted Andrew, 'they didn't want to overdo it!'

'Anyway, I'm here because Jack didn't fancy doing this presentation thing with – what's his name? Mr Abbott. Jack's the quiet, peace-loving type. I'm ...' He looked at Ronan. '... not.'

So, Andrew had begun the presentation with a series of questions. They'd planned the way to start to get a laugh, but the wild, frenzied laughter was out of proportion to the joke. The whole class was edgy. The earlier projects had been listened to with impatience. Most had chosen to hand in folders. They were all waiting to hear Andrew and Jack's account of the hit-and-run incident. And every time Mr Abbott used Jack's name, 'No Brains' sniggered.

First, Andrew described what he thought it was like to

live there before the cars came: 'My gran says there was only one man in Avondale Road who could drive. And he didn't have his own car. He'd been taught to drive by the bakery where he worked. So even he didn't have a vehicle parked outside his house. What was the road like then? It was like a park outside every child's house …'

Ronan was staring at Jack intently, but, in contrast, Bunny was leaning against the wall listening nonchalantly. He had his arms folded at the beginning, and, as one tedious presentation had followed another, he appeared to have sunk into a stupor, but as the boys' theme developed, he showed signs of interest. He unfolded his arms, stopped leaning against the wall, and then started to nod vigorously as they made their points. They would have been encouraged by this, if they hadn't known what was coming …

Jack took over the presentation. He tried to stand a bit more upright than usual so the gang would notice a difference in him, but he warned himself not to overdo it. He didn't want anyone else asking questions. 'That meant:

1 Children were safe. Their parents could keep checking them, but probably didn't have to, because there were no cars to worry about.
2 Old people could get about. They could move across the road as slowly as they needed to …'

'Animals could too!' chipped in Colm.

But Jack and Andrew had planned how they were going to introduce this subject and now was too soon.

'What that meant,' said Andrew, 'was that the road was a *community*. The old people had a chance to see the young ones, keep them in order. And because they knew each other better, they cared more.'

Now Jack took over again and showed the graphs they'd made from the figures. Number of cars parked in the road – every space was filled. Number of cars driving through the road – up to eighty an hour.

'All speeding through,' continued Andrew, 'cutting the community down the middle. It's called rat running, and it causes all sorts of problems.'

He paused. This was where he and Jack had planned that he should tell the story of Rosalind. The class was listening intently; so was Bunny. 'For example, it means old people can't go out …'

'You've said that,' complained Ronan, listening more carefully than he usually did in any lesson.

'And there's nowhere to play.' Andrew stopped and looked at Jack.

'Is that it?' asked Bunny. 'You don't seem quite sure whether you've finished.'

Jack knew he could not risk hesitating, because Jasper wouldn't. 'We think the way cars dominate our environment is dangerous and makes car drivers selfish,' he said. 'People drive through too fast and think it doesn't matter what damage they do!'

'We wanted to show these photographs of what the road was like before cars,' added Andrew.

He started handing round the faded photographs. Bunny leaned forward and looked at each one as it came his way.

'What happened to Andrew's gran's cat shows how cars make people selfish,' persisted Jack. 'Last week, a driver hit a cat and didn't even stop!'

'Yeah, cat-killer!' muttered Colm.

'I see,' said Bunny quietly. He had just taken another photograph and was staring at it. The colour drained from his face. He stared as if at a ghost.

There was silence. Not even Ronan stirred. Looks passed between all the boys.

Then Bunny seemed to shake himself awake. 'I think I can see where this is heading.' He paused, then asked, 'Do you know who ran over the cat?'

Jack and Andrew, still standing at the front of the class, remained silent.

'Jack!' It was Bunny's voice.

'No Brains' sniggered.

'Andrew seems lost for words, so I'm asking you. Do you know who ran over the cat?'

'Yes, sir!' A bold answer from Jasper, bolder than Jack could have managed.

'What evidence do you have?'

'Whoever hit the cat lost at least part of his numberplate. We know that.'

'I see,' said Bunny. He didn't shout; he seemed extraordinarily calm, as he went on, 'I don't think it's escaped the attention of any of you that my front numberplate has been missing.'

No response from the class.

'My numberplate has been missing since Wednesday evening. When did your gran's cat get run over, Andrew?'

'Last Wednesday, sir.'

'At what time?'

'About four, sir.'

Mr Abbott's tone was that of counsel for the prosecution; Andrew's was that of a very reluctant witness.

It's as if he wants us to think he's guilty, said Jack to himself, as the bell rang.

The double lesson was over.

'You're not usually reluctant to depart this room!' said Bunny grimly, as the class stared at him. 'Class dismissed!' he barked. He still held the final photo in his hand. Neither Jack nor Andrew dared ask for it back.

As the quickest of them reached the door, Bunny added, 'Oh, and barring a masterpiece in the projects handed in, Andrew and Jack have won the prize. Well done, the two of you.'

22

Little Ray

By the end of the school day, Jack was exhausted. So that Ronan and Co. thought he was new to the premises, he had to follow Andrew about. He couldn't even look as if he knew which desk to sit at. He realised that Penrock College wasn't new territory any more. He was actually getting quite comfortable in the surroundings, and now he had to pretend it was his first day again! Progress or what?

As soon as they had left the geography room, the whole class started talking about Bunny's reaction.

Colm ran up to Andrew and Jack. 'He did it all right! Did you see the way he looked when you said about the cat? Why don't we wheel-clamp him?'

'Yeah,' 'No Brains' added, 'and he's giving you the prize as a bribe.'

'As a bribe for what?' objected Andrew. He was really miserable now that Bunny had been shown to be guilty.

'It's your gran's cat,' said Ronan. 'I worked it out first,

remember! He's trying to make sure she doesn't do anything about it. Report him or something.'

Jack was about to say that running over a cat was an anomaly and he'd told Ronan that before when he remembered that it had been brother Jack who had imparted that information.

As soon as school ended, Mr Abbott sped away, so his BMW was spared wheel-clamping for one day, but Jack and Andrew knew that Ronan and Co. would be looking for retribution.

They headed towards Avondale Road disconsolately. The success of Jasper's day was offset by the discovery of Bunny's guilt. They now had two problems – what to do about that and worrying about Cuthbert's next move. Jack still expected to see a police car outside number 60.

Instead, as they neared Gran's house, they saw Bunny's BMW parked outside!

Andrew stood in horror. 'I'm for it now!' he exclaimed.

'What's he doing here?' asked Jack. He was still trying to accept that Bunny was capable of running over a cat and not bothering to stop. But what now? Andrew seemed to think the teacher was there to get him into trouble, but Jack realised the teacher would contact Andrew's parents, not his gran. Was it possible that he had come round to apologise?

'Come in with me,' urged Andrew.

Jack would have liked to go straight home, but Andrew had stood up for him when he was new and friendless. He had to stand by him now. 'OK.'

Andrew used his key and entered. Jack followed right behind him. Andrew didn't shout out as he usually did. They listened. They could hear voices in the sitting room.

They went in and found Gran hovering over Bunny, who was sitting on the sofa! Samson was weaving between his legs and Rosalind was on his lap! They stared.

Bunny was the first to speak. 'Ah, your grandmother has been telling me what a help you are to her.'

The boys said nothing. Jack noticed that Bunny was smiling, but all the worst villains in James Bond films were like that – smooth, plausible. Surely he wasn't capable of something even worse than what he had done already?

Then Gran said, 'Look who's come to see me – Little Ray!'

She was holding the photograph that Bunny had kept in class. She showed it to Jack and Andrew. It was the picture of girls playing in the street. 'See? That girl holding the rope? That's Ray's mother, my best friend.'

Gently Mr Abbott took the picture from her. 'Yes, that's my mother,' he said. 'Seeing a photo of her in the middle of a geography lesson was quite a shock, I can tell you.'

'So, your mum lived around here?' asked Andrew.

'She lived next door. My mother was Rosalind Cuthbert before she married.' He stroked the cat on his lap. 'It's nice to think her name has been carried on.'

'But that makes Cuthbert your uncle!' said Jack.

'Precisely! Which explains why I was visiting next door

on Wednesday,' explained the schoolteacher. He was still smiling, as if he was unaware that he was owning up to being in Avondale Road when Rosalind was run over.

Jack and Andrew stared at him. The loathsome Cuthbert's nephew – a family of drunks and villains indeed!

Bunny saw the look on their faces. 'I will have that tea you offered,' he said to Gran. She shuffled from the room. 'I think I need to explain something to you.'

Jack was tempted to say, 'Go ahead!' but even if they were out of school, he decided he had better not push his luck.

'Sadly, my mother died recently,' explained Bunny. 'She left me some money. Her brother, whom I hadn't seen for many years, summoned me round to discuss the matter. For some reason, he seemed to think he was entitled to some of his sister's money. She had left him nothing in her will, knowing he would only drink it away. Well, the meeting did not go well. He was abusive and threatening.'

'We often hear him shouting through the wall,' added Andrew.

'I'm sure,' said Bunny. 'At one stage, he rushed outside. I stayed, trying to calm his wife, who is a much more reasonable person.'

Jack thought about Mrs Cuthbert handing Frank Rosalind. Being stuck in a house with a drunken bully like Cuthbert was even worse than being bullied at school.

Bunny continued, 'He'd grabbed my car keys and

started the car. I'd spent some of the money my mother had left me on that car, and that seemed to enrage him. I had to force him to stop the car. He did so, reversing into his own gate in the process.'

So it had been Bunny's car, but not Bunny at the wheel! Both Jack and Andrew were grinning.

'I knew about the damage to my car, but knew nothing about Rosalind here being injured. My uncle must have hit her when he started up my car. She must have been lying concealed somewhere when I rushed out.'

'Then, after you left, he went out and took her in!' said Jack. 'My mum saw Cuthbert take Rosalind inside, but it was you she heard drive off. She can't see very well without her lenses, you see,' he explained. 'Actually, she's as blind as a bat.'

'I see!' said Bunny, smiling. He was drinking the cup of tea Gran had brought him. 'So,' he said briskly, 'I hope that clears matters up, and that I won't find further pieces of my car disappearing!'

Andrew and Jack found themselves nodding. Did they have something to tell the class!

'Thank you for the tea, Mrs Lynch. Allow me to pay for Rosalind's treatment.'

Gran shook her head. Jack wasn't sure if she understood the part Little Ray's car had played in Rosalind's injuries. She seemed to regard his being there as just an overdue visit from her childhood friend's son. 'No, no, Ray. It's very nice of you to visit.'

'I'll come again, if I may,' he said kindly. 'I've had a lesson today about community feeling and I won't forget it.'

'Keep the picture of your mother, Ray.'

The boys watched him leave.

'Wow!' said Andrew. 'Wait till we tell Ronny!'

23

Secrets

Jack ambled across towards his house. Things were beginning to work out. Penrock College was no longer an alien place. The best teacher wasn't a hit-and-run driver. In fact he was 'Little Ray', nice to old ladies and with an embarrassing relative. And Jack almost felt sorry for Ronan when he thought about how they were going to reveal the Jasper joke on Monday – almost. He wouldn't be too hard on him, but he reckoned that if he wanted to, he could get Colm and 'No Brains' to deposit Ronan in a dustbin!

He sauntered in, thinking he'd give Frankie a call – tell him that Cuthbert had been guilty. But he wouldn't ask for any more of Frankie's bright ideas. He could sort things out for himself. Jasper bounded up to him and Jack patted him as they went into the kitchen.

Mum and Dad were sitting in silence. Dad was smoking a cigarette and exhaling the smoke painfully.

'What's up?' Jack asked.

Mum wiped away tears with a hankie.

'Come on!' said Jack cheerfully, but he got no response. 'What, has someone died?'

Mum began to cry, while Dad scowled at Jack. 'You've really upset your mother,' he said accusingly.

'Me? I haven't done anything! I've just come in,' objected Jack.

'Have you told everyone you ...' His mum looked as if she was going to cry again. 'Have you told people in school that you have an identical twin brother?'

Dad answered the question Jack had been asking himself. 'A lad came to the door asking for Jasper – your identical twin, Jasper!'

'Was it someone called Ronan, or did he have glasses ...?'

'What does it matter who it was?' shouted Dad in exasperation. 'Did you say it?'

'I could have died,' said Mum. 'He asked to speak to you, and when I said you were out, he asked to speak to Jasper. I thought it a bit odd that he wanted to *speak* to the dog. I went to get Jasper, and that's when this boy said, "No, I mean Jack's ... Jack's identical ..."' Mum could manage no more and rushed upstairs, crying.

Dad looked furious, and Basil and Jasper moved around Jack in intricate patterns, a sure sign that they had picked up the atmosphere.

'Sorry,' tried Jack. 'I just had a bit of bother at school.'

'What sort of bother makes you say you've got a brother?' shouted Dad.

How to explain, wondered Jack. Mum and Dad seemed to live in an infinitely safer world than his. Nobody threatened Dad in the street or called Mum a smartarse because she knew how to cook a roast dinner. He hadn't started at Penrock College *planning* to invent Jasper!

'I don't see why Mum's so upset,' Jack complained. 'I know it was a lie, but I haven't killed anyone!'

Dad sighed and called up to his wife, 'Marie, come down if you can.'

Slowly, Mum descended the stairs. She gave a little smile as she came back into the kitchen. 'It just brought it all back,' she said to her husband.

Dad said softly, 'I'm going to tell him, love. Sit down, Jack.'

Dad had made him sit down when he'd told him they were moving to the city. Dad preferred to flee – preferably in his Golf – when things got emotional. Now, he lit another cigarette and inhaled strongly before he said, 'That's the problem, Jack. It isn't a lie. You had a twin brother, an identical twin brother.'

Jack realised something at that moment. He realised that deep down you can know something that nobody has ever told you. It can be a secret, deliberately hidden, but somewhere inside you, you know it anyway. When Dad said, 'You had an identical twin brother,' Jack said to himself, Of course! He's the one I miss all the time.

He had lots of questions and Mum and Dad answered them. They spent the evening talking about what they had concealed for so long. Their twins – boys – had been the first in the family, and there had been great excitement, especially as they were identical. But there had been complications before the birth. Both Jack and his brother had been ill. His brother had been called Delgar. Before they were a week old, Delgar died. At first, it had been too painful for Mum and Dad to talk about, but then they had decided that Jack would miss his brother if he knew, so the rest of the family had been asked not to tell.

All the people he knew best – his aunts and uncles, his cousins – had all kept it from him. Wasn't it a sort of lie, he wondered, to conceal something so important? They'd say it was to protect him, he knew, but *his* lie had been to protect himself too, and they didn't seem too keen on that!

And not telling me hasn't stopped me missing him, thought Jack. Now he knew who he had missed all his life. His brother was coming into focus.

'Am I the younger one?' he asked.

'No,' Mum had answered. 'Delgar was younger. He was smaller than you and weaker.'

So he hadn't got that right. There was no bigger, tougher brother. If Delgar had lived, Jack would have had to look after him.

By the time he went upstairs to his bed, Jack felt exhausted. It had been a busy day, so busy that he'd forgotten to tell Mum and Dad that he had found out exactly what had happened to Rosalind, and he had won a prize at school.

Even though he was tired, it took a while to get to sleep. He lay awake, imagining Delgar sleeping on the bunk beneath him. The rhythmic sound of Jasper's snoring had never seemed so sad before ...

24

The Egg

Monday, as Jack walked under the wrought-iron arch of Penrock College's main entrance, he thought back to when he had started at the school. Then, he'd been totally over-awed by the size of the place. He hadn't known what the motto meant – and he still didn't. Judging by events so far, it probably said something like 'It's going to be tough, but who said life was easy?' One day he'd get round to asking someone.

He could ask Andrew. He had a friend now, but today they had other things to do. He'd probably tell Andrew about Delgar sometime. First he had Ronan to sort out. That had been made easier by the discovery that Mr Abbott was innocent. *Wrong again, Ronny!*

Jack was glad anyway. He admired Little Ray. Explain-ing that you're related to the neighbourhood drunk couldn't be easy, but Bunny had managed it. Jack was beginning to think he preferred Bunny-type solutions to

Frank's. He hoped Frankie wouldn't get totally wheel-clamped one day.

He wondered what the prize for the project was going to be. Even if it wasn't great, it meant Mum and Dad would get a good report about him on parents' evening.

The only problem he had left was that he had missed rehearsals of *Annie Get Your Gun*. How had he managed to get himself involved with that enterprise? Like a lot of things, it had made sense at the time.

Then Jack remembered that Andrew had been keen to join him at the auditions. Perhaps it wasn't too late for him to get a part. After all, he was a TV star. The drama teacher would be really pleased. If he turned up with Andrew, he'd probably get away with forgetting a few rehearsals.

Jack saw Andrew waiting for him in the distance and waved. He was looking forward to telling his friend how he thought they should break it to Ronan that he'd been tricked into believing in a non-existent twin brother.

Jack checked his schoolbag. It contained a carefully wrapped raw egg. When Ronan found that on his chair, he'd begin to realise it was not going to be his day.

ALSO BY CREINA MANSFIELD

MY NASTY NEIGHBOURS

David and his family are typical – three messy, noisy teenagers; two tidy, organised parents. It just doesn't work, does it? But when Mum inherits some money, they find a solution: *two* houses, one next door to the other. Now they can live separately, teens in number 8 and parents in number 10. What could be better? At first it seems like paradise, but then things begin to go wrong …

Paperback £3.99/€5.07/$6.95

CHEROKEE

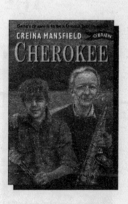

Gene's grandfather, Cherokee, is a famous jazz musician and Gene travels the world with him. He loves the life and his only ambition is to be a musician, too. But Aunt Joan is totally opposed to the idea and insists he live a 'normal' life with her. Is this the end of Gene's dreams, and what is really behind his aunt's hatred of music? Escape seems the only option – but life is often more complicated than it seems, and life has a lot of surprises in store for Gene.

Paperback £5.47/€6.95/$7.95

ALSO FROM CREINA,
FOR BEGINNER READERS

SNIP SNIP!

Panda Number 18

Erin loves to cut things with her little scissors. She cuts out paper dolls to play with. One day she cuts her hair and Mum is very cross. But Erin can't help it, she just loves to go *Snip Snip!* Cutting things can cause lots of trouble, but then she finds out that grand-dad loves cutting things too ...

Paperback £4.33/€5.50/$4.95

OTHER BOOKS FROM
THE O'BRIEN PRESS

THE JOHNNY COFFIN DIARIES
John W Sexton

Twelve-year-old Johnny Coffin is a drummer in a band called The Dead Crocodiles, goes to school with the biggest collection of Murphys in the whole country, and has a mad girlfriend, Enya, who has a man-eating pet. Johnny chronicles the problems of being twelve, like his teacher, Mr McCluskey, who is trying to destroy his mind with English literature.

Paperback £5.47/€6.95/$7.95

CALL OF THE WHALES

Siobhán Parkinson

Over three summers, Tyke journeys with his anthropologist father to the remote and icy wilderness of the Arctic. Each summer brings short, intense friendships with the Eskimos and incredible adventures: Tyke is saved from drowning and hypothermia, joins a bowhead whale hunt, rescues his new-found Eskimo friend, Henry, from being swept away on an ice floe, and witnesses the death of innocence with the killing of the narwhal or sea unicorn.

Paperback £5.47/€6.95/$7.95

THE LOST ORCHARD

Patrick Deeley

Paul Duggan, aged eleven, lives in tiny, rural Darkfield on the borders of the beautiful and mysterious wetlands, known as the Callows. Strange planes are seen flying over the village, and a mining company starts buying up the land to turn it into an open-cast mine. Only old, eccentric Magpie O'Brien opposes the mining. Paul must find the courage to stand up to the school bullies and to this new threat to his way of life. Will the mine bring wealth and happiness, as the villagers hope – or ruin and death?

Paperback £5.47/€6.95/$7.95

BENNY AND OMAR
Eoin Colfer

Benny is a young sporting fanatic from Wexford. Hurling is his reason for living; his family is his reason to practice advanced sarcasm! Then Benny is forced to leave his beloved Wexford, home of all his heroes, and move with his family to Tunisia! How will he survive in a place like this? This crowd have never even *heard* of hurling! Then he teams up with local-boy Omar, and a madcap friendship between the two boys leads to trouble, crazy escapades, a unique way of communicating and heartbreaking challenges.

Paperback £5.47/€6.95/$7.95

Send for our full-colour catalogue
